Leaving Fletchville

Leaving Fletchville

RENÉ SCHMIDT

ORCA BOOK PUBLISHERS

Library and Archives Canada Cataloguing in Publication

Schmidt, René
Leaving Fletchville / written by René Schmidt.

ISBN 978-1-55143-945-7

I. Title.

PS8637.C44915L42 2008   jC813'.6   C2008-903060-5

First published in the United States, 2008
Library of Congress Control Number: 2008928580

Summary: Brandon has a reputation for being a big dumb bully, but when a new
family comes to town, he works hard to protect them and keep their secret.

Orca Book Publishers gratefully acknowledges the support for its publishing
programs provided by the following agencies: the Government of Canada through
the Book Publishing Industry Development Program and the Canada Council for the
Arts, and the Province of British Columbia through the BC Arts Council
and the Book Publishing Tax Credit.

Design by Teresa Bubela
Cover artwork by Getty Images

ORCA BOOK PUBLISHERS
PO Box 5626, STN. B
VICTORIA, BC CANADA
V8R 6S4

ORCA BOOK PUBLISHERS
PO Box 468
CUSTER, WA USA
98240-0468

www.orcabook.com
Printed and bound in Canada.
Printed on 100% PCW recycled paper.
11 10 09 08 • 4 3 2 1

*To all my students who had to be the adult when they got
home, especially those of you I never knew about...*

Acknowledgments

My first thanks go to my sweet Shirley. Without your unselfish efforts all year long, I would never have time to write. This book is yours too. And thanks to my late mother-in-law, Marg, who loved the whole thing. A fatherly hug to my sons, Adrian and Dan, for encouragement and dialogue tips. I am especially grateful to Aileen Fletcher, who invented Fletchville, a program that has been well used by me and my classes for many years. Thanks to Bev Donaldson and Barbara Trimm, who shared valuable insights. Thanks also to Lindsay Wiginton for grocery store secrets. I am especially grateful to all my students for their great suggestions: Jayden Adams, Josh Anderson, Zach Baarda, Mackenzie Born, Sommer Boyce, Tori Deline, Jesse DeWar, Patrick Earle, Steven Foster, Jessica Labelle, Kaitlyn Lebell, Jennifer MacDonald, Courtney Main, Zack

Makarchuk, Chris Maxwell, Andrew McColl, Haley McRae, Kaitlyn Noble, Forrest Oldreive, Emily Osmond, Blake Richardson, Lauryn Ronsky, Cameron Sager, Cole Sager, Brennan Thompson, Josh Thompson, Ben Worobetz, Anna Barker, Holly Doxtator, Taylor Forth, Jake Grimmer, Cassie Hackett, Jesee Jones, Travis Jones, Ryan Lafleur, Roisin Larcombe, Robin Lidster, Vicki MacDonald, Ryan McGale, Nathan Niles, Dallas Ohl, Adam Olson, Jonathan Pidoux, Taylor Rodden, Morgan Scott, Ben Squier, Michael Trus, Donnie Wallace, Mac Willock and Scott Woodbeck. If I can do it, you can too. Keep writing!

Finally, a big thank-you to Sarah Harvey, who chose the manuscript and did such a great job editing it. You made it happen.

Chapter One

The day Leon came to my school was a day like any other. I was in the principal's office again for disrupting the class. It had all started when Mrs. Cawfield asked Zach where his homework assignment was. As usual, Zach's hair was unbrushed, and the collar of his shirt was stained. He'd worn the shirt for three days in a row. He swallowed, and a muscle jumped in his skinny neck as Mrs. Cawfield asked him again for his homework. There was fear in his eyes. Anyone could see that he didn't have the work done. What Mrs. Cawfield didn't know was that when Zach got in trouble at school, he got beaten at home. With fists. I never did my homework. Most teachers had stopped asking me for it.

"Zachariah, where is your assignment? It is overdue."

I waited until Mrs. Cawfield looked away so I could whip an eraser at Roger's head.

"Hey!" shouted Roger as he turned to look behind him.

"Roger!"

"Someone threw an eraser at me!" Roger was grinning. He liked this kind of disturbance.

"Okay. Who's throwing erasers in my classroom?"

I turned in my seat as if I was looking to see who the eraser thrower was. I made a loud fart noise as I turned. Most of the class laughed. I was just warming up.

Mrs. Cawfield turned to me. "Brandon. Was that you?" Mrs. Cawfield was old, and her patience was wearing thin. She probably would have been happier as a librarian.

"Pardon?" I asked.

"You heard me. Was that you?"

"Was what me?"

"Did you make that noise?"

"Noise? What noise?"

And so it went. Finally she did what she always does—she sent me down to the office. When I got there, a little kindergarten girl named April sat with an ice pack on her elbow, waiting for her mom to take her home. Her legs swung as she looked at me with wide eyes. I was the school bad boy. "My" chair was vacant. Everyone knew that the center chair was "Brandon's Chair." It had a Brandon-shaped dent from my butt being in it most days. It should have had a brass plaque.

The secretary, Mrs. Miller, sighed when she saw me. "What is it today, Brandon?"

"I dunno."

"Did Mrs. Cawfield send you down?"

"Nope."

"Then who sent you?"

"I forget."

"Isn't this the time of day you get kicked out of Mrs. Cawfield's class?"

"Oh yeah. That's right. Mrs. Crawfield." I repeated the name like I'd never heard it before. "Crawfield. Yeah. She sent me down. Forgot her name for a second."

"Cawfield, not Crawfield," said Mrs. Miller, sighing again. "Even you ought to know her name by now."

"What's that you're doing?"

"Pardon me?"

"What are you doing with those buttons you press?"

"Typing. On a keyboard," she said slowly as the principal, Mr. Sitzer, came out of his office. Mr. Sitzer was in his late forties with a bad comb-over. Today his pants had hanger wrinkles. He stopped smiling when he saw me.

"You must be pretty busy today," I said.

"Pardon me, Brandon?"

"You must be pretty busy, Mr. S."

"Why do you say that?"

"Well, I've been out here about twenty minutes. Usually you call me in faster."

"Brandon, do you have any idea how much work I have to do without dealing with you and your persistent opposition to authority?" Mr. Sitzer was trying to look like a tough guy. It didn't work. He was shorter than me, and he looked flabby.

"Per-per-sissy-tant? Are you calling me a sissy, Mr. Sitzer?"

"Of course not. Don't change the subject, Brandon."

"But you started it. You called me a…"

He reached for the phone but didn't pick it up. "I don't have time for this. I'll call your parents later. You will spend the morning in the office—an indoor suspension!" Mr. Sitzer leaned forward, trying to make it sound like a terrible punishment. I smiled at him. His hands trembled as he reached for a pen.

"He gave me an indoor suspension," I said to Mrs. Miller, like I was proud of it.

"So he did." She sighed and went on with her work. I settled in for the usual boring day in the office, but that was the day Leon George and his family came to my school.

Chapter Two

You can tell a lot about people by their shoes. Josh has a field car he drives around on his grandpa's farm. The heel on his right shoe is wearing down from driving so much. Mr. Fletcher, my math and history and drama teacher, rides a motorcycle, and you can see the worn spot on his left toe from where he shifts gears. All long-time bikers have that worn spot. Ricky wears skateboarding shoes because he shows off on his skateboard all the time. Skateboarding shoes are pretty much useless for anything else. They have stiff soles, so they don't bend very well. Running in them is like running with boards on your feet. Sometimes I chase Ricky just so I can see him run funny.

The first thing I noticed when Leon came into the office that day were his shoes—nothing flashy or expensive. Just plain runners. No thick soles. His shoes looked as if they'd be good for all kinds of things, and they were worn in evenly. Leon had them laced up all the way and double knotted. Nobody who gets around much leaves their laces loose or untied. Loose shoes come off when you are climbing, kicking a ball or fighting. Leon saw me looking at his shoes. He looked at mine. They were a lot like his: inexpensive, worn in and laced all the way.

"Those people have black faces," whispered April, still sitting and dangling her legs off the edge of the chair. That was the second thing I noticed about Leon and his family. They were black. They stood out like chocolate chips in vanilla ice cream. Most of the people who live here are white. It's not a rule or anything, but there just aren't any black people. A few Asian people, but no black ones. I sat and watched Leon and his family register for school and wondered how they ended up in a boring little place like Kingsville.

If you want to listen in on a conversation without being noticed, do something with your hands. Fiddle with your watch or take apart a pen or bounce a ball if you have one handy. Listening while sitting still with your head tilted toward someone is a dead giveaway. While I listened to what was going on in the office, I carved my initials into the sole of my shoe with a multi-tool I always carry.

Leon was my height or even taller, which would make him the tallest kid in school. He had broad shoulders but was thinner than me. He and his sister were quiet-spoken, and their clothes were clean but old. The sister, Winnie, was tall too, and pretty. She looked older than the other grade seven girls, and Leon seemed mature for an eighth grader. Their little brother, Sam, looked to be about ten. His mouth was stained from his orange pop and there was a smear of peanut butter on his cheek. He was the type of kid who needed a grandma-style spit-wash. He was scowling. His pockets bulged. He probably collected all sorts of useful stuff, like I used to. He started kicking, gently but steadily, against the leg of the office chair next to mine. Leon whispered to him to stop. Sam stopped for a few seconds. Then he started up again.

Their dad spoke quietly to the secretary. He wore steel-toed boots. Construction worker, I figured. He looked older than my dad and kind of rough, like he'd forgotten to shave for a few days. He didn't pay much attention to Sam as he answered Mrs. Miller's questions.

Yes, they'd just moved to the area. No, they didn't have a phone yet, but they would have one soon. The kids' previous school was in Toronto.

"Are you sharing custody with another parent?" Mrs. Miller asked.

"No. Their mother is deceased."

"I'm sorry," said Mrs. Miller. I didn't hear the dad's mumbled reply.

"What is your full legal name?" Mrs. Miller turned to Leon.

"Leon Andrew George."

"Date of birth?"

Turned out he was a year younger than me, even though he looked older.

"What is your full name?" Mrs. Miller asked Winnie.

"Winnifred Elizabeth George."

"Date of birth?"

Winnie was only twelve. She looked at least fourteen.

While all this was going on, Sam snuck a laser pointer out of his pocket and shone the little red dot at a mirror that hung on the back of the closet door in the office. Then the laser dot danced on the ceiling. Then it appeared on Mrs. Miller's forehead. Winnie snapped her fingers quietly, gesturing for Sam to give it to her. He hesitated before handing it over, like he was worried he would never see it again. Winnie slipped it into her jeans' pocket.

Sam started looking for something else to do. He saw April sitting beside me, staring at him. He made a cross-eyed face at her. She stuck her tongue out at him.

"What is your address?" the secretary asked Mr. George.

"Thirty-five Tobermory, apartment 411," he answered. I blinked. Thirty-five Tobermory was my address too. It's a four-story apartment building near the train tracks. It isn't the fanciest place in town. In fact it's the crummiest. They must have moved into the empty apartment on the fourth floor. Leon would be in my homeroom class and in my building. So I offered to show them around the school. It just seemed like the right thing to do.

"No thanks, Brandon." Mrs. Miller frowned. "In case you've forgotten, you're serving an indoor suspension." Even if I hadn't been, she wouldn't have trusted me with a burned-out match. That was my reputation: big and dumb and disobedient. I am not really disobedient. I just don't like being told what to do. I never did. Not at home. Not at school. People say I was first kicked out of school after just three days of kindergarten…but it's not true. I left on my own.

The day after Leon came to our class at Kingsville School, it was meltingly hot and nobody wanted to do any work. All they did was watch the new kid while pretending not to. As if they had never seen a tall black kid before. Maybe some of them hadn't. Leon was ignoring all the attention, but he probably hated being stared at. Most people do.

"Uh, Mrs. Cawfield," I said in the middle of English class. "Mrs. Cawfield. My dad says it's rude to stare. Is he right?"

"Well, of course, Brandon. You shouldn't stare."

"Well, Mrs. Cawfield, when I stand up like this and put my foot on my desk, everybody stares at me."

I stood and put my foot on my desk to retie my shoelaces. The class laughed.

"Brandon. Sit down now."

"But I have to tie my shoelaces. They're loose. And now everyone's staring."

"Brandon. Sit down now."

"And if I stand on a desk, like this, that's against the safety rules, isn't it?" I stood up on top of the desk. By now the entire class was staring at me, open-mouthed. I bounced a little. What kind of idiot would stand up on his desk in the middle of class? Everyone was laughing now. They probably figured I'd finally lost my mind.

"Brandon. Get down immediately," Mrs. Cawfield shrieked. I could see she was close to losing it. No sense pushing her over the edge. I sat down.

"Brandon. You'll have to go down to the office. I can't have you standing on desks. Explain yourself to the principal."

"Okay," I said. I spent the next few hours sitting in the school office, listening in, pretending to be too stupid for anything and learning quite a bit. Several girls in grade eight were caught smoking on the school bus. The superintendent wanted some report Mr. Sitzer hadn't finished yet, and there was a head-lice problem in the grade five class. Business as usual at Kingsville School.

The next day in Mr. Fletcher's history class, I sat behind Cassie Doucette, who has really long hair. Cassie was one of the smart girls in my class and probably the prettiest. Unlike the snobby girls, she never treated me like I had rabies or something. Maybe she even liked me a little bit. I was bored, so I began braiding her hair using four bunches at a time, which didn't work at all. I was going to try five bunches, but Cassie pulled away and whispered, "Don't tangle it up."

While I was busy braiding, I watched Leon, who was listening to the lesson about the American Revolutionary War and the Loyalists. He actually seemed to be interested. How anyone could care about something that happened more than two hundred years ago was beyond me.

Mr. F. was going on and on about how Loyalists who served the King of England and fought against the revolutionary forces were awarded land. "Many of them settled in this part of Ontario," he said, "and also in New Brunswick and Nova Scotia. Even people who were employed by the government or those suspected of not wanting to fight, even though they supported the cause of freedom, were sometimes branded Loyalists and chased from the United States. Usually they lost land, houses, possessions—everything but their lives."

I found myself wondering how people could allow themselves to be kicked around like that. How do you let someone take your job, your land and your house?

It seemed to me you would fight back or something. Then I remembered seeing movies about Jewish people being taken by trains to camps in Germany where they were made to strip naked before they were sent to gas chambers. Also I remembered a TV show about a guy named Idi Amin, who might have been another Hitler, locking up a bunch of people in Uganda. Maybe if the whole country is against you, you can't fight back.

Was I thinking about history? I gave my head a shake. Time to move on to more important daydreams.

Chapter Three

Recess was my favorite part of the school day. In fact, recess was the only good thing about being in an old-fashioned K-8 school. There were no shop rooms or science labs at our school. We didn't have a decent-sized gym or fancy change rooms like the junior high in Springfield. All we had were classrooms, a tiny gym and lots of little kids getting underfoot.

Kids in grade seven and eight were not actually supposed to have outside recess. Sitzer threatened to take it from us whenever there was too much rough stuff, but like most of his threats, he never followed up. So at recess we went out when the little kids did and played sports in our part of the school yard. I wasn't into sports much, so I hung around. Usually a bunch of little kids followed me, hoping they'd get to see me walk on my hands or do one-armed push-ups.

That hot day after history class, I was entertaining them by pretending I could squeeze a soccer ball until it exploded. I made my face go purple as I squeezed the ball, but really I was busy watching what was going on with the new kid, Leon. He was leaning against a wall in the shade when Ricky Skelton, from the other grade eight class, came over to check him out. Ricky was like a deerfly. You didn't know he was on you until you felt the bite.

Ricky wore his baggy jeans real low like someone from a big-city gang. He and his friends liked to act tough. I figured if he ever saw a real gang member he'd pee his pants and lock himself in his mom's Mercedes SUV. Ricky led his little gang of followers up to Leon.

"Hey, new guy, you play basketball?"

"Not much," said Leon.

"I bet you've got all kinds of cool moves."

Leon glanced at Ricky's baggy "gangsta" pants and looked away.

"Serious, man. Not my game," Leon said.

A crowd had gathered, and Leon saw everyone watching him.

"I don't play basketball," he said again. Ricky picked up a basketball and bounce-passed it over to Leon. I kept pretending to destroy the soccer ball, but I walked closer to see what was going on. The gang of little kids followed.

"Bwandon can bweak anything," a toothless little grade one boy said. Meanwhile, I was watching, hoping

Leon would kick Ricky's butt. Ricky was a good athlete, but he bragged too much.

"I said I don't play," said Leon. He passed the ball to Ricky. I could see Winnie looking over at him from the sidelines.

"One-on-one! One-on-one!" kids started chanting.

Ricky began showing off. He dribbled around, faked a shot, turned, jumped and did a nice lay-up. He caught the rebound and passed it to Leon, who took the ball clumsily, dribbled twice and tried a hook shot. He missed the backboard and almost took a girl's head off.

Ricky picked up the ball and made some more deft moves, deking around Leon, who made no move to intercept the ball. Ricky shot again. A perfect swish.

Leon took the ball again, dribbling past Ricky, who grabbed the ball neatly and sank it again. After three more tries at shooting, Leon had barely hit the backboard. Ricky had scored five baskets.

"You really *don't* play much basketball, do you?"

"Nope," said Leon.

"I thought all black guys played basketball," Ricky said.

Leon's face froze. "This black guy doesn't," he said. There was something hard in his voice.

"Be cool, man," said Ricky.

"Cool?" Leon paused and looked at Ricky for a few seconds. "I'll show you cool," he said. He walked past

Ricky and through the group of kids who had gathered around.

"He walked away. What's so cool about that?" said Ricky to his friends, who all laughed. "He's a black guy who can't play basketball." They laughed some more.

"Don't be an idiot, Ricky," said Cassie. "Why should he have to know how to play basketball just because he's black?"

When Mr. Fletcher came by, Ricky and his friends stopped talking and studied their shoes. Racist comments were not allowed at our school. Nobody knew for sure whether Ricky had crossed the line or not, but after Mr. Fletcher moved on, Ricky started in again. "I guess the black man can't jump," he said. His little gang snickered.

"Watch this," I said to my group of followers. No teachers were nearby. I walked over to where Ricky and his friends were shooting hoops and sat down directly underneath the basketball net, hooking my arms around my knees and closing my eyes.

"Uh, what are you doing, Brandon?" Ricky asked.

"Shhhhhhh!" I said.

"Brandon, you big goof, we're trying to play basketball," said one of his buddies.

"Ten…nine…eight…" I counted loudly, ignoring them.

"Brandon. We're trying to play a game here," Ricky said. He was trying to sound tough, but everybody knew he wouldn't dare take a shot and hit me with the ball.

I continued to crouch. "Seven…six, um…six, um… four…"

"He can't even count backward, he's so stoopid," whispered one of Ricky's friends. I ignored him.

"Four…um…five, three…two…one…KA-BOOM! I'm a time bomb!" I shouted as I jumped up and knocked them all over. Bodies went flying all over the place. I fell on Ricky and one of his cronies. "Oooops!" I said as my elbow dug into Ricky's ribs. "'Scuse me. I'm just getting up."

All the little kids who had been watching laughed. Unlike the older kids, who thought Ricky was so cool because he was rich and good at everything, the little kids didn't seem so impressed with him. Maybe they were pretty smart in their own way.

During lunch break, Ricky came up to Leon in the school yard.

"Hey, new guy. What's your name?"

"Leon," said Leon. He looked wary.

"Leon. What kind of name is that?"

"It's a good name. What's yours?"

"It's Ricky. Now, Leon, how do you spell that? Is it L-E-O-N?"

Leon nodded.

Ricky smiled. "Like Leon's Furniture?"

"I guess," said Leon.

"Not related?"

"It's my first name. The furniture people, it's their last name."

"But it's a different name—Leon. Not from around here. It's Noel spelled backward, isn't it?"

"I guess."

"Were you born at Christmas and your parents didn't know how to spell?" Ricky's friends laughed. "Just kidding," Ricky added quickly.

"No. My parents named me for my grandfather."

"But your name is Noel backward, though." Ricky and his buddies laughed again.

Leon's jaw clenched shut.

"What's wrong?" Ricky said. "You got something against me? I'm just trying to be friendly with the only black kid in the school, and he isn't being friendly back."

Leon walked away. It was the second time he had turned his back on Ricky. I wondered how long it would be before Leon fought back.

Ricky had come after me on my first day at the school when I arrived in grade five. He was interested in me only because I was the biggest kid in our grade. I thought he was being friendly until he started showing off for his friends by pushing me to fight. While he was taunting me, he kept glancing over his shoulder at a teacher who was on duty nearby. I guess he thought it was safe to act tough because the teacher would prevent a fight. He guessed wrong. It took two teachers and the custodian to pull me off him, and his black eye and bruises lasted longer than my three-day suspension. But it was worth it. Ricky and his friends never bothered me again. Neither did anyone else.

Chapter four

Zach Kerr had been absent from school for two days in a row. Some kids picked on Zach because he was skinny and weak. He had stringy hair and his teeth stuck out so much he looked like a rat. Last year he had fainted at school one morning, and the rumor was that he never had breakfast. When our school got a breakfast program, a lot of kids just came in for snacks, but Zach, who needed it, never went. Maybe he was too embarrassed to go. But it was unusual for him to miss school.

Zach and his weasel-faced dad lived in the same building as me and Leon, on the ground floor. Instead of a balcony, they had a small porch leading onto a scruffy lawn beside the back parking lot. Years ago it had been a nice apartment building, but as time went on it looked more and more worn down. Zach's dad left empty beer bottles and old car tires and appliances on the back porch, which didn't improve the look of the place.

When he wasn't drinking, Zach's dad was a carpenter. My dad says he was one of the best in the business, but he was a mean drunk, and he wasn't well liked. Some summer days I would go out behind the apartment building and lean against the wall by the laundry room. I would sit in the sun and observe the neighborhood. I could hear when things were getting bad at Zach's apartment. His old man's voice would get louder and louder the drunker he got. If an adult came by, he quieted down. Sometimes my ball hitting their back window was enough to distract the old man, and his shouting turned to mumbles and curses. Once, when my dad heard noises inside Zach's apartment, he banged on the door to ask if everything was all right. That sobered Mr. Kerr up in a hurry. Last month someone called Children's Aid to report Mr. Kerr's abuse. They visited, but nothing much happened. Mr. Kerr promised to sober up, and Zach didn't have any bruises for a while. Nobody ever found out who made the call.

The second day Zach was absent, I made sure I got kicked out of class and was in the office as Mrs. Miller called the homes of the kids who were absent. I pretended to fall asleep on my chair. It wasn't comfortable, so I lay down on the floor.

"Brandon. *What are you doing*?"

"Sleeping. I'm kind of tired."

"Well, you can't sleep on the *floor*! "

"Where should I sleep then?"

"You were sent out of class. Do you not have any respect?"

"So I can't sleep at all then? How about in Mr. Sitzer's office? Can I sleep in there?"

"Absolutely not! Does this look like a hotel?"

"All I want to do is sleep…" I replied.

Mrs. Miller got up and knocked on Mr. Sitzer's door. "Mr. Sitzer, Brandon is lying on the floor of the office. He doesn't listen to anything I say. Can't you do *anything* with him?"

"I'm busy here. Please deal with it, Mrs. Miller."

She whispered something, and I heard her hiss the word *suspension*.

"Mrs. Miller, I have the superintendent coming in five minutes. I can't deal with Brandon right now."

Mrs. Miller came back to her desk, just about slamming the principal's door. I grinned and pulled myself up onto the chair and pretended nothing had happened. She glared at me and jabbed angrily at her computer keyboard.

A few minutes later she called Zach's home and left a message for his dad. After she hung up she wrote *NA* beside Zach's name. I could see what she wrote from where I sat. Reading upside down is another trick I've learned during my many days in the office. After a minute I asked, "What does NA mean?"

"Excuse me?" she asked.

"What does NA mean?"

She looked at me like I was crazy. "Why do you ask?"

"You wrote NA on your list."

"Brandon, first—don't read things on my desk. Second—NA stands for No Answer."

So Zach wasn't answering the phone. I hoped he was okay.

As I walked through the hallway to the washroom, I saw Ricky and his little wolf pack coming toward me. I sauntered into him, ignoring the others, and made sure I stepped, heel first, on the toe of his fancy hundred-dollar Circas. I dug my heel in a little as I went by.

"Oops! Sorry," I said with a fake smile.

"Hey, watch where you're going, Brandon." Ricky was always braver when his friends were watching. But he also should have remembered that I *never* back down, no matter who is there—friends, relatives, teachers, principal, police. I walked back and stood with my heel on the other shoe.

"Pardon?" I said quietly, breathing my stinky garlic breath into Ricky's face from about two centimeters away.

"Just kidding. You can step on my toe whenever you want, Brandon." The way Ricky said it, it still sounded funny. His friends laughed. I walked away.

After school I went to Zach's apartment and knocked on the door. I heard a noise inside, but there was no answer. I called out, "Zach, are you there? It's me, Brandon."

I heard more noises, and Zach finally came to the door. He tried to hide it from me, but his left eye had those greenish yellow patches around it that you get when a black eye is healing.

"Wanna sleep over tonight?" I asked.

"Um, I'm not sure," Zach muttered.

"No, you can't." Zach's dad's voice came from somewhere in the apartment.

Zach's face fell. "I ca-can't," he mumbled.

"I was going to watch the Leafs' game," I said.

"No. I can't," Zach said again.

When I got home, my dad was just getting up. When he's had a late trucking run, he usually sleeps all day the next day.

"Can I have a friend sleep over?"

"If it's all right with Mom, sure. Just don't wake me up tonight. I have to leave early tomorrow."

"His dad won't let him."

"Then he can't go. Respect people's rules, Brandon."

"But it's Zach, the boy in 114."

My dad glanced at me sharply. "That Kerr guy? His son?"

"That's him. I want Zach to come over, but his dad says no."

"His dad beating him again?"

"I don't know. Maybe," I said.

"Is that what this is about? You don't normally have kids over."

"Maybe," I said again.

"I'll see what I can do." My dad put a shirt on, combed his hair and went down the stairs to the first floor. My dad hardly ever takes the elevator. He says he needs the exercise. I followed him down. He knocked on the door of apartment 114. Zach answered the door, and my dad gave him a friendly grin. I stood back a bit, watching.

"Can I talk to your dad?" my dad asked.

In a minute, Zach's dad's weasel face came to the door. He looked badly hungover.

"Mr. Kerr? I'm Brandon's dad. Now I know Brandon has already asked your boy over, and you said no. And I respect that. But I want to reassure you that Brandon's mom and I will be at home all the time. The boys won't get into any mischief."

Zach's dad hesitated. My dad stepped a little closer to him. He had a way of talking to people that made them pay attention.

"Your boy will be safe with us," Dad continued. "We're just upstairs, you know. Why don't you write down the phone number?" He smiled as he talked, but there was no smile in his eyes as he looked at Mr. Kerr.

"I guess he can go," mumbled Zach's dad. "He got in a bit of a scuffle the other night with some lads down at the gas station. I told him he was grounded, but I guess if you want him to come so badly, I'll let him out of my sight for a night." Mr. Kerr struggled to look sincere.

"Sure," said my dad. My dad was not somebody to mess with. Mr. Kerr knew that. I get my size from him. I must get my attitude from someone else, because my dad is a stickler for following rules.

I don't often see my dad real angry, but once in a while he can get pretty steamed. The summer I was ten, he took me with him on one of his runs in his truck. We were at a truck stop near Saskatoon. One of the waitresses had a blotchy birthmark on her face, like a big red stain all across her cheek. It looked pretty bad, but she was nice. Dad knew her by name—Dorothy or Doria or something—and she knew him and called him Stan. She served us pancakes and gave me a free Coke. We were just finishing when a guy sitting at the counter started in on her.

"These eggs are too runny. I can't eat this snot." Only he didn't say "snot."

"I'll get the cook to do them a little more," Dorothy or Doria said.

"Yeah, and make it snappy," he said.

"It'll just be a few minutes," said the waitress. "The chef is kinda backed up…"

"Don't get all red in the face now, dearie, but I want my eggs done the way I like 'em and I don't wanna wait."

The waitress slowly put a hand to her red blotch, and tears came to her eyes.

It got pretty quiet in that restaurant. My dad stood up and told me to wait in the truck. I pretended to go, but I waited by the door to see what he would do.

My dad went up to the guy who had insulted the waitress and put his big left hand on the man's shoulder. His fingers tightened. He picked up the man's plate of eggs with his right hand and held it in front of the man's face. He leaned down and whispered something that nobody else could hear. The guy turned to look at him, and he went white. The guy called the waitress over and apologized to her. All the while my dad was standing with his hand on this guy's shoulder and his other hand holding the plate. Nobody messes with my dad.

Zach came to our place, and we watched the Leafs' game. That night he slept on my mattress on the floor while I slept on the box spring. A few times he yelled in his sleep.

Chapter five

The town of Kingsville is small and plain. It has two main streets that cross at a set of traffic lights. The downtown area is made up of buildings that don't match each other. The bank is an ugly flat-roofed building made of glass and stainless steel. Next to it, the old bank building, with its huge pillars and fading cement lions, has been made into the library and community center. The post office is another old building with lots of steps down the front. The grocery store is new and modern. My dad says that businesses in Kingsville make most of their money in the summer when the tourists come to the park to go camping by the lake. There are a few small strip malls farther along the highway, but there's no big mall to hang around in. The only all-night donut shop was built from an old gas station. It still looks like a gas station from the outside. People say the donuts taste like gasoline. Teenagers and old men hang out there. The town hall and courthouse building is new. Next to it is the arena and a park. There are two new subdivisions in town. Vinyl villages, my mom calls them. She says lots of retired people live there, making their lawns and gardens perfect by spraying them with poison. My parents moved here because the pollution in the city made my mom's allergies worse, but she is still sick a lot.

The town should have been built along the lakeshore, but it wasn't. I don't know why. It looks like the town fathers tried to hide the shoreline the way you would hide a gravel pit or a dump. The lakeshore lies beyond the two-lane shore highway and a small hilly field littered with weeds and road trash. The shore has small stretches of sand and larger areas of rocky beach. The lake is usually too cold for swimming until the very end of summer, but it's a great place for bonfires. In the summer there are lots of beach parties, at least until the police show up and send everyone home. Most of the adults stick to the boring main streets of town—the grocery store, the post office, the parking lots. Us kids cut through the field to the shoreline and walk along pathways by the beach. Even with the weeds and trash, it's a nicer way to walk than through the streets of Kingsville.

Leon walked home that way sometimes. He walked slowly, like someone in trouble who is avoiding going home. One day I saw him stop at the rocky part of the beach. With a piece of driftwood that looked like a club, he began picking up rocks and batting them into the water. Like a baseball coach hitting fly balls, he kept batting rocks into the water, over and over, for at least half an hour. He never seemed to get tired. Toss, swing, *thwack*. Over and over again.

Another day I watched him bicycle over to the bulk grocery store. He used the plate glass window as a mirror, grinned at it to check his teeth, buttoned his shirt higher and went inside. Within two days, he was working there. I wondered how he did it. Last year I'd asked for a job, but they told me I had to be fourteen. This year, even though I was old enough, I didn't bother.

Our apartment building looks over the town. It is the highest building in town, even though it is only four stories tall. Our apartment is on the second floor, on the side facing the lake. The rent is pretty cheap, and my dad can park his tractor-trailer in the lane beside the parking lot.

Every night after my mom goes to work at the hospital, I am like the unofficial night watchman. When everyone else is inside, watching TV or going to sleep, I walk around. I go through the hallways, watching and listening. I know who is getting along and who isn't; I know when people come and go. Nobody seems to notice when I make my rounds, but I can tell you as much about people in our building as the building superintendent—and probably more.

My patrolling also takes me outside, through the different residential neighborhoods and the downtown area. I used to pretend I was a spy. These days I pretend I'm a superhero. With my size and strength, I'm like those guys who patrol bad neighborhoods, like the Guardian Angels in New York City. My mom says I should become a cop. Whatever I become, I'm better than most people at noticing stuff without being obvious. I had already noticed a lot about Leon.

Leon and his family had been living in our building since late September. According to the neighbors, their mother had recently passed away from cancer. Leon's dad owned an old Buick but didn't use the car; the dust under it was building up. When I walked by their apartment, it was always quiet. Sometimes I would hear a TV in the background, and sometimes I heard talking. There were never any loud sounds. Winnie began babysitting for people in our building who had little kids. The three of them came and went from school, and sometimes I'd see Leon playing catch or road hockey with Sam in the back parking lot. Leon would throw easy balls for Sam, who was left handed and clumsy at catching. Leon would also let Sam score on him in road hockey.

One warm day I was sitting in the school office again. I was down for the usual complaint—not cooperating with the teacher. (It really wasn't my fault. I didn't like Mr. Fletcher's attitude, and I told him so.) While I was sitting there, Sam was brought in by a yard-duty teacher.

Sam had already been in trouble at school a few times. Trouble followed him around like a hungry dog, just like it followed me. Sam looked a lot like Leon, only smaller and with green eyes. Today his face was smeared with dirt, which looked gray on his black skin, and he had been crying. His knuckles were skinned, and another crying grade four kid came with him. The other boy had bruises on his face and knuckle marks on his cheek. There were rips in the knees of their pants and holes in the elbows of their shirts. Sam's sleeve was half ripped off. They'd obviously had quite a battle before the teacher had stepped in.

"He started it!" they both yelled, pointing at each other.

The teacher, Mrs. Langhammer, sighed, smiled wearily at the secretary and told the boys to wait for the principal. She put them on either side of me, where they sniffled and rubbed their bruises. Sitzer called them in one at a time and talked to them with the door shut. At one point he came out and asked the secretary to look up Sam's father's work number; apparently their home phone number was not in service. Mr. Sitzer called our class on the PA to get Leon down to the office. Leon arrived and glared at his brother.

"What is your dad's work number, Leon?"

"It should be the number in your records."

"It isn't, and no one answers at your house."

"Apartment."

"Apartment, then."

"It's out of service," said Leon.

Mr. S. sighed. "Can you pass this message on to your dad? Sam was fighting. He didn't start it, but he was pretty hard to stop. The rules are clear: we have a no-touch policy on the playground. Fighting usually gets a suspension. He'll have to spend the rest of the afternoon in the office. If it happens again, I'll need to have your father in for an interview."

"I'll pass on the message," said Leon. He shot a steel-eyeball look at Sam. I wondered why it was such a big deal. Little boys fight. It clears up misunderstandings.

Leon shouldn't have worried. I'd figured out that Mr. Sitzer was even more afraid of parents than he was of the school superintendent. Usually Sitzer gave kids an "indoor suspension" so he wouldn't have to deal with angry parents. Mrs. Miller hated it, but it kept the parents off Mr. S.'s back.

After school that day I saw Sam outside playing his usual game of catch with Leon. Whatever trouble Sam had gotten into, he hadn't been grounded. That's what my dad usually does if he finds out I've been fighting. It doesn't do me much good, but it makes him feel like he's done something, I guess.

Chapter Six

Most kids liked Mr. Fletcher, our math and history teacher. He was funny. Before he became a teacher, he had traveled around the world for several years, working on ships, cooking in restaurants and hitchhiking. He explained things by telling interesting stories, unless kids like me were acting up. Then he was strictly business, especially the strictly part. I never could fool old Fletcher.

One day he announced a new type of weekly assignment for our math class.

"You kids are going to learn how to take care of yourselves. Every Friday we are going to pretend you live in a make-believe town I call Fletchville. You will be living and solving problems as if you were twenty-five years old. You will all get jobs and earn money."

"I want to be rich," shouted one kid.

"I want to be on welfare," laughed another.

"You will pull a job out of a hat, and that's what you will do. No changing jobs, no quitting. Every day you are at school will be like an eight-hour day at your job. Some of you will be well-paid and some will be paid just enough to live on. The challenge for you is to pay all your bills and still have money left."

"Where do we live?"

"You will begin at your parents' houses, but each week's assignment will help you become independent enough to move out into your own places."

"What if we want to live at home?"

"Remember, we are assuming you are twenty-five years old. You won't want to be living at home when you are twenty-five."

"How are we gonna save up enough?"

"Wait and see."

The first week, we each pulled a job out of a hat. There was one doctor, one lawyer and one dentist. They earned lots of money, but the rest of us had ordinary jobs, like cashier or cook or bus driver. I was a plumber. I did pretty well. After paying taxes and bank loans for my tools, I would be taking home about eleven dollars an hour. Leon was a cashier, which paid minimum wage. We had to calculate how much pay we earned every week by multiplying the amount we earned per hour by eight hours in a day, then by the number of days we had been in school that week. If you were off sick, you lost a day's pay.

I never usually bothered doing math. Most days I just doodled in my notebook, but this assignment sounded sort of interesting, so I got out a calculator. I would make $88.00 a day and $440.00 a week if I was at school for five days. Four hundred and forty bucks sounded like a lot of cash. Leon would make less—320 bucks a week—as a cashier.

A week went by and I entered my first week's pay on my balance sheet, the way Fletcher showed us. I had a bank balance of $352.00. I hadn't made the full $440.00 because I had skipped school one day, and Fletcher remembered it. "Uh-uh, Brandon. You were absent Wednesday, so you only had a four-day workweek."

The next week I made sure I wasn't kicked out of class, and I didn't skip out either. We had to learn about groceries: how much it would cost to buy food for your twenty-five-year-old self for one week. The assignment said that even though we were still living at home, our fake Fletchville parents were getting tired of us never paying for groceries. So we had to go to the store with a list and find out what things cost. It had to be healthy food too, which made it less fun. I stuffed the assignment into my book bag, where I usually leave all my assignments.

"Ah, Mr. Fletcher?" Cassie asked.

"Yes, Cassie?"

"Can we use coupons?"

"Absolutely. That's a great way to save money."

Leon started writing a shopping list on his sheet. I leaned over and read what he'd written: *Brown bread $1.29 a loaf, Milk $4.39, Cheese*—he tapped his teeth with his pencil for a moment—*Mozzarella Cheese $1.39 for 400 grams.*

"How do you know all those prices just like that?" I asked.

"I work in a grocery store," he said. "This is easy," he added without looking up.

Well, it wasn't easy for me. As usual, I asked my mom to help me with it, and, as usual, she said I should do it myself. Most times, that was where I stopped working and handed in nothing. But this week was different. This was interesting, even if it was going to cut into my time sitting around and watching the world go by.

I went to the grocery store with my list and tried to find all the foods I like. I wasn't sure where Doritos fit on the Canada Food Guide, and steak was expensive. Eggs were all sorts of prices depending on the size, and the brown ones were more expensive. I wasn't sure why. Leon walked by with a mop and a bucket. He was wearing an apron and a red shirt, like all the employees at the store.

"Leon."

He stopped.

"How many potatoes do I need for a week? In Fletchville."

"What do you mean?" he asked.

"I'm trying to figure this out. How much to pay for everything. Like potatoes." I felt stupid asking for help.

Leon shifted the mop handle from one hand to the other. "How often do you eat potatoes in a week?"

"Maybe every meal. I like 'em," I replied.

"So you probably eat about half a bag. Maybe."

"Maybe. So how much do I pay?" I asked.

He pointed the end of the mop handle in my direction. "You want me to do your Fletchville assignment for you? I'm working."

I liked how he stood up to me. Either he hadn't heard about my bad-guy reputation or he didn't care.

"Just tell me how to do it. Then I can do it myself."

"Okay. Fletcher wants you to figure out what just one week of groceries would cost, right?"

"Right," I said.

"So you figure a bag of potatoes costs about three bucks, right?"

"Right."

"So you divide three dollars by two. That'll make a buck fifty for a week of potatoes. Write on your list *Potatoes $3.00, divided by two, equals $1.50*. Get it?"

"I think so."

"Do that with bread, milk, cheese…whatever you eat."

"Do I divide it all by two?"

"No, you doorknob. First figure out how long it takes you to go through something. Like a loaf of bread.

If it takes one week to eat a loaf, then you need one loaf. Don't divide it. If it takes two weeks to eat, like a box of cereal, divide by two. If it takes three weeks to eat, like a turkey, divide by three."

"Why does he want us to write it all down?" I asked.

"He wants you to explain your thinking."

"You buy your stuff here, don't you?"

"I get a discount."

"Can you get stuff free?"

"Only if they are going to throw it out," he said. "I'm not supposed to, but they don't say anything."

"Why would you eat food that's gone bad?" I asked.

"I don't. I only get stuff that's old but still good, like day-old bread. People are fussy and won't buy it."

"You like saving money, don'tcha?"

"Does a bear crap in the woods?"

"So back to the groceries, how do you know if stuff is fresh?"

"Sometimes by smell," he said. "I smell my potatoes before I buy a bag."

"You smell your potatoes?"

"Come here," he said. We walked down the vegetable aisle to where the potato bags were stacked. He picked one up and sniffed at the little window in the bag. "Smell that."

I smelled it. "Smells like dirt."

"That's good. If there's a rotten potato in there, you'll smell it. Never buy a bag if there's one rotten one in there. It'll stink up your whole place and rot the whole bag."

"What else can you tell me?"

"Do you like oranges?"

"Yup."

"Then pick them out one by one—don't buy a bag. Hold each one in your hand and give it a little squeeze. A good orange is heavy; it means it's juicy. It's also got a bit of give when you squeeze it. That means you can peel it easy."

That Friday I handed in my Fletchville assignment with the rest of the class. Mr. Fletcher held it up and looked carefully at it. "Is this yours?" he asked.

"Yup," I said.

"I think I'll frame this, Brandon," he said, loudly enough for the whole class to hear.

"Why? Is it that good?" I was surprised. Nobody had ever framed anything I had done. My mom used to stick my art projects on the fridge when I was little, but that was about it.

"It's the first complete and on-time assignment I've ever seen you do. That includes all last year when I taught you science and health."

Everyone laughed, but I still felt good somehow. Maybe next week I would hand something else in.

Chapter Seven

Most days after school, I saw Leon go to work at the store. On weekends he was there pretty much all day. I wondered what he did with his cash. He probably had more money than any of us, but he was careful not to show it off. In fact, when we had two-dollar dances after school, he never went. Or when they sold pizza lunches on Fridays, he brought his usual bag lunch. Once or twice when someone left an apple behind because they didn't want it, Leon would pick it up when he walked by. He never made it obvious. Later I would see him eating it. He didn't play sports much, unless you counted playing catch with Sam or walking with Winnie and her friends. Winnie wasn't as quiet as Leon. She liked to laugh, and she had made lots of friends at school already.

In the evening, when other kids were watching TV or playing Nintendo, Leon was rotating stock and carrying grocery bags. How he ever got his homework done was a mystery, even to me. Unlike me, Leon did his best to stay out of trouble. His head would nod in class sometimes, and once he even fell asleep, but he always had his homework done.

Winnie was a good student and a hard worker, but she also had a reputation as a joker. When the music class sang together as a choir, she sang really well—loud and in tune. But whenever the teacher came closer to hear who was singing so well, Winnie started singing off-key. The teacher didn't know what to make of it. Finally one of Winnie's friends told the teacher who it was, and the teacher was really impressed. Apparently it is a lot harder to sing off-key when you do it on purpose. I wouldn't know, because I don't sing—off- or on-key. The teacher encouraged Winnie to take some music lessons, but she said she was too busy.

After about a month of Fletchville assignments, such as figuring out the cost of buying new clothes for working in our pretend jobs and finding out how much it cost to do laundry, most of us had earned enough money to move out of our parents' houses. We had a thousand or so bogus dollars in our fake bank accounts. We were supposed to find ads for places we could afford. We had to have enough money for the first and last month's rent. The other kids seemed to understand why, but I was having trouble with the concept.

"What's the deal with first and last month's rent?" I whispered to Leon one day in class.

"When you first move in, the landlord asks you for an extra month's rent for the last month you live there."

"Why?"

"He doesn't want you moving out some night and stiffing him for a month's rent."

"How do you know all this stuff?"

Leon laughed. "I pay attention to Fletcher. You should try it sometime. He's explained it half a dozen times!"

Cassie asked, "Can we share with somebody? Save on rent?"

"Great idea, Cassie," Mr. Fletcher replied. "You may share with as many people as there are bedrooms in your apartment. In other words, a three-bedroom apartment can have three of you in it; a two-bedroom place can have two only, etcetera, etcetera."

"How about if someone sleeps on the couch?" asked Roger.

"Nobody sleeps on the couch. When you're twenty-five, you'll want your own bedroom."

The students quickly decided which of their friends they wanted to share an apartment with. Nobody approached Leon or me. Leon looked over at me and asked, "Are you in?"

"Sure," I said.

"You want to check the want ads for apartments?"

"How about our building?" I suggested.

"No way!" we said at the same time and laughed.

"Too ugly," he added. We agreed we could find a nicer place to live.

That fall, Kingsville was famous for a little while. People in town got calls from friends and relatives all over the world asking what was going on in Kingsville. Anyone watching CNN saw three passenger cars and a diesel engine burning on the train tracks just outside town. Serious-sounding news anchors said as many as twenty people might be dead inside the train cars. But I hadn't just watched it on TV. As usual, I was right there and had the best view.

It was already dark, and I was behind our apartment building when I heard the passenger train on its way to Montreal. Same time as always: 8:00 PM. There was a loud bang, and I could hear the train coming closer, but a strange rattling sound came with it. Then the brakes began to squeal.

It looked like the regular passenger train, but there was a glow around it that I'd never seen before. Orange flames blew out of the car right behind the engine, covering the sides and bottom of the train and lighting up the windows. Black smoke billowed back from where the flames ended. I could see passengers in the second and third cars running to the windows to see what was happening. Above all the noises, I thought I heard screaming. Fuel was pouring out of the big tanks underneath the locomotive and spraying back over the rest of the train. A woman was silhouetted against one window, looking out and down. She looked at me for a second, and I could see she was really scared. Under the train, the tracks were on fire too, as big puddles of fuel covered the rails and ties.

Within a few more seconds the rattling, banging, burning train had zoomed off down the track and was out of sight, leaving pools of burning fuel on the tracks. It was as if a giant comet had flown by. I could hardly believe what I had seen. Yes, I had seen a burning train go by. The stink of diesel fuel and fire stayed in the air. Behind me I heard balcony doors open. Half our building came out onto their balconies, trying to see what was happening.

"Brandon. What's going on?" someone yelled.

"What are you up to?" shouted the superintendent. As usual, he suspected me of something.

"The train's on fire. It just went down the tracks," I shouted. Leon leaned out of his balcony on the fourth floor. "Come on, Leon. Let's go check it out!"

He hesitated. Then he shook his head.

I ran to my bicycle. The train was gone, but the pools of fire lit the tracks ahead like a bunch of burning tires. Maybe the train would stop somewhere nearby.

Only kids like me knew there was a bicycle path that ran along the railway line for miles. Soon I was racing down the familiar path, which was almost too dark to see. The stink of diesel fuel engulfed me as I rode, and here and there patches of flames leaped off the tracks. When the train tracks passed over the road at the next level crossing, I saw a larger fire. In the middle of it lay a two-meter-long piece of bent steel rail. I could see the train about a kilometer ahead, still burning. The fire siren began to wail from the fire hall, calling the volunteer firemen from their TVs and night jobs.

When I had pedaled about a kilometer east of town, I caught up to the train. By now the fire lit the whole area around the front of the train, while the back half was still dark. The sound of sirens blared from the highway, which was about a football field away to my left. I knew that none of the fire trucks or ambulances could get close to the burning train. There were no roads leading to the tracks, just little pathways made by kids.

The back of the train seemed fine, but the stink of diesel fuel and smoke from the fire hung in the air. Passengers were coughing and stumbling along the tracks, many of them bleeding and some of them limping. Lots of them weren't wearing shoes, and they didn't seem to know where to go.

"Where is my newspaper?" moaned a woman, limping up to me. Her face was covered in soot.

The whole sky behind them was glowing like sunrise. I could see clearly by its light. In the last passenger car, several men were being carried down the stairs and put into wheelchairs. Another man, in a train company uniform, was talking into a walkie-talkie.

"We're getting the wheelchair basketball team out now. Out."

"Where are you taking them? Out."

"We're moving them away from the train and off the tracks. I can hear the sirens to the north of us. I think there's a road back there, but no way to get to it that I can see. Out."

"Hey, mister," I interrupted.

"Who are you?" he asked.

"I live near here, in Kingsville. There's a path back there that leads to the highway." I pointed back toward the town.

"Hey, Larry." The man clicked the mike on his walkie-talkie. "I've got a local kid here. Hang on."

He turned back to me. "Is that how you got here?" he asked, looking at my bicycle.

"No, I took a different path along the tracks. This path leads to a house on Highway 2."

"That's what we need. Show me the way." He clicked his radio on again. "Larry, this kid's on a bicycle, says there's a path to a house on the highway. I'll keep you posted. Out."

"Sure, Salim," came the voice. "There's a whole lot more injuries. People jumped from windows and some of them are cut up pretty bad. We need to get them some help. Out."

I led the man along the tracks and then back about ten meters from the crowd of passengers. As we went farther into the darkness, I started to worry that I wouldn't be able to find the right path. I could hear Mr. Davis, the owner of the nearest house, start his old tractor. Just as I found the path, the headlights showed he was crashing through the bushes toward us. People back on the tracks cheered as the tractor slowly widened the path through the bushes toward the train tracks. More headlights in the distance showed the fire department had come up the Davis driveway, and ambulances were coming in behind them.

I led some injured people to Mr. Davis's house, and his wife took them inside.

"What happened? Are you all right?" she asked as she led them in. In the light I could see their pale soot-smeared faces and torn clothes.

For the next hour, firemen dragged equipment toward the fire while people bundled in coats or wrapped in blankets stumbled into the house, hardly able to see in front of them. Many were limping, and one or two had to be carried. The wheelchair basketball team needed some help over the low spots, but they were okay otherwise. Volunteer firefighters from town, including my old soccer coach and the pharmacist, came with lanterns and firefighting equipment.

I felt like I was in a war zone. There was so much going on, my hands began to shake like I'd had too much coffee. I hate to show excitement or fear or anything, but it was hard to stay calm. All this time, the front two cars of the train continued to burn. Kids who lived along the highway came by on their bicycles to watch. Some of them tried to help, but they just got in the way. Pretty soon the police sent us all back and away from the tracks. There were flashing lights everywhere. Radios crackled with messages from emergency vehicles and mixed with the sounds of motors idling and generators running, adding to the general confusion. A big crowd had gathered on the Davises' front lawn.

"I was here first," I told the kids I knew. "I saw it all."

Soon a helicopter came from the air force base and *wop-wopped* overhead as it shone a searchlight on the train. It was so loud you could hardly hear anything else.

I had never seen so much happening all at once. Even for someone like me, who's used to watching what was going on, there was too much to take in. I sat on an ambulance bumper and just stared. Before long, a uniformed railway cop came up to me. A man from town had pointed me out.

"What's your name, son?" he asked.

"Brandon."

"Brandon what?"

"Brandon Clifford."

"What do you know about this fire?"

"Nothin'."

"My men say you were first on the scene."

"Yeah."

"Yeah? What else do you know about this fire?"

"Nothin'."

"Okay, cut the crap and give me good answers here. How did you get here so quick?"

"On my bike."

"From where?" he asked. I sensed he was getting ticked off and decided I'd better tell him what I knew. "I saw it from town. The train was burning."

"Where do you live?"

"Kingsville."

"Where in Kingsville?" I gave him my address. He got out a little book and wrote down my name and a few notes. "So why did you put the rail on the tracks?"

"What? I never…"

"There's a piece of rail on the tracks. Why did you put it there?"

"I never put anything on the tracks." I started getting nervous.

"Sure you did. Big fat piece of rail. Right in the middle of Kingsville. Might be a lot of fun to see a train derail, right?"

"I never did that," I said.

"Why did you put it there?" he repeated.

"I never did." I'd been blamed for lots of things before, but this was the worst.

"The engineer saw kids over on the tracks."

At this point, my old soccer coach saw what was going on and came over.

"Everything all right?" he asked.

"Who are you?" demanded the cop.

"Kingsville Fire Department."

The man in uniform snorted. "Volunteer? Thanks, but I'm with the CN police. Some kid put a section of rail on the tracks. That's what caused all this. Probably killed a few people."

"This boy's okay. I'm sure he didn't do it."

"Why do you say that?" asked the CN guy.

"I doubt Brandon would do something stupid like that…something that would hurt people," the coach said, but then he began to look doubtful.

"This is a crime scene, my friend. We'll start with whoever we find," said the CN cop.

He questioned me a lot more, and I had to give my phone number, which he checked with someone he called on his cell phone. Finally he let me go, and I pedaled home. For once in my life I told my mom and dad what had happened and what I had been accused of. It was worse than anything I'd been accused of before, but even my dad asked if I had done it. That hurt, but at least he believed me when I said no. He said not to worry, but by that time I was pretty freaked out. He knew what time I had gone out, and when I told him what time the accident happened, he said we had proof of my innocence.

At first nobody knew how many people had been on the train, and the police and firemen thought some of them were missing and presumed dead in the first and second passenger cars. As it turned out, all of the passengers were finally accounted for. Nobody got fried in the train cars.

For weeks afterwards, the burned-out coaches sat on a siding in town, and investigators asked all kinds of questions and took a lot of pictures. It turned out some older kids had been seen putting a section of rail onto the wooden ties, sticking one end up over one of the steel rails. The idiots thought it would be funny to stop the train, but it punctured a fuel tank and then ripped through a section of electrical wire, which shorted out and ignited all the fuel that had leaked out. Those kids ended up in the juvie detention center and on the news, but no one ever interviewed me, thanked me or apologized for accusing me.

Chapter Eight

I was a bit of a celebrity at school after the train fire. Word got around that I had been there and seen the whole thing. Life went back to normal after a while, and I returned to the role of big dumb observer.

One afternoon the school yard was more empty than usual at lunch because a lot of kids were rehearsing for the school talent show. It was a big deal at our school. Usually the newspaper sent a reporter to take pictures of the winner. One or two kids had even been featured on the local TV station. Ricky was going to play his electric guitar again this year. Like most things he did, he played really well, which made him act like more of a jerk than usual.

That day, he was outside at lunch with his little band of followers. I stood nearby, and Ricky gave me a few suspicious looks but carried on talking about a big party he had had the week before. Lots of kids from our class had been invited, as well as some of the older-looking grade seven girls. I wasn't invited—not cool enough, I guess. Winnie had been invited but she hadn't gone. Winnie came out of the school with a group of her friends just as Ricky was bragging that he didn't need to rehearse any more.

"Hel-lo hel-lo," Ricky said, staring at her as she walked by. "You should have come to my party last Friday. You could have had a good time."

"What kind of good time?" Winnie asked suspiciously.

"Oh, the usual. Good music, good food…" Ricky looked to see if any teachers were nearby, "some beer, a bit of smoke…"

"I'm allergic to smoke."

"I mean grass smoke. You ever tried it?"

"I knew what you meant," said Winnie, "and I said I'm allergic."

"How about beer? Do you drink beer?"

"I'm not old enough to drink, and neither are you." Winnie smiled.

"My mom lets us," said Ricky.

Winnie smiled sarcastically at Ricky. "Well, doesn't that make you such a *big* boy…" Her friends laughed.

"What do you do for fun, Winnie?" said Ricky, staring at her tight-fitting jeans.

"Not what you have in mind…" Winnie said.

"I don't believe that. Besides, I like colored girls," Ricky said.

"Colored? Who's colored?" Winnie turned back to him with a wicked grin.

"Well, you are, aren't you?"

"Now Ricky, when you go to the beach and sit in the sun for a while, what color do you turn?"

"Tan—brownish—I guess," said Ricky.

"And if you stay in the sun too long, what color do you become then?" continued Winnie.

"Red. What are you getting at?"

"How about dead white people? What color are their faces?"

"Gray. Like, you should've seen my grandfather after he died. He was—"

Winnie interrupted. "Suppose you white people are sick from the flu and you're ready to puke. What color are you then?"

"I don't know—greenish?"

"Ever see someone with jaundice?" continued Winnie.

"What's jaundice?" asked Ricky.

"When your liver shuts down. White people look yellow when that happens."

"So what's your point?"

"You just made my point, Ricky," laughed Winnie. "You white people can be white, brown, red, gray, green or yellow. Black people are always black. So who's colored now?" Winnie's friends all laughed.

Ricky laughed too. "That's pretty good, Winnie. Did you just make that up?"

"No, I read it somewhere."

"You're cool." Ricky reached out to Winnie and grabbed her as she began to walk away. "Stay. I want to talk to you some more," he said.

Winnie pulled his hand off her arm. "You're *not* cool," she said.

"Hey, I said I wanted to talk to you some more." Ricky grabbed her arm again.

"Let go of me," she warned him quietly. Her smile was gone.

"Stay longer." He pulled her toward him.

"Don't touch me!" she hissed at him and wrenched her arm free.

Ricky was quiet for a moment as he watched her walk away.

"Now that's cold. I'll have to work on her some more," he said as he turned back to his friends and continued with his story.

"So then yesterday, like I said, we were on our skateboards, and the cops came up to us and said to move it 'cause we were on private property." Ricky did a few spins on his skateboard. "Mike, my brother, said, 'My uncle owns this property and he lets us ride here. You cops are the ones who are trespassing.'"

"He said that?"

"Yeah, he did. Said it right to the cop. I was laughing so hard…"

"What did the cop do?" asked one of Ricky's friends.

"He said something about bylaws and ordinances and all sorts of other bull. Mike just laughed in his face and said, 'You want to come talk to my uncle? He's right inside.' It was great."

"So what happened when the cops came to the door?"

"My uncle gave them a hard time," Ricky said. "We were standing right there."

"So what did he say?" asked one of his gang.

"He told them to leave us alone. They've got no business telling us to go. We're minors, and they can't touch us." Ricky did a few more tricky spins on his skateboard. "They can't tell us what to do," he said. "It was the same cops who came to my house about the missing four-wheeler. My mom really gave it to them that time."

Ricky's mom was always telling everyone how innocent her sons were. Last year she defended Ricky's brother, Mike, even after grass was found in his locker. She said it was planted there by someone else. Lately she had been complaining that Ricky's teacher was marking him too hard. He'd started the year in our class with Mr. Fletcher, but she'd had him transferred out because she claimed Ricky was getting unfair treatment. I think Mr. Sitzer was afraid of her. She was a big bleached blond who wore too much makeup. She'd come in and complain about something a teacher had caught Ricky doing, and usually Ricky wouldn't get punished. Mr. S. knew if he did punish Ricky, his mother would call the superintendent.

I was getting bored listening to Ricky. Some little kids came up to me, so I winked at them and whispered, "Watch this." I made sure there were no teachers looking, and then I started making a sound like a jet warming up, throttles full out, brakes on, getting ready for a blast down the runway. I spread my arms out and ducked my head down. I began my takeoff roll down the parking lot runway, all my engines screaming. Ricky and his buddies were still in a group, all four of them.

I ran up to them with my arms wide open. "Clear the runway!" I clotheslined them all, and we fell in a heap on the ground.

"Brandon. What are you *doing*?" shouted Ricky.

"Hey. I'm a fighter jet. I had a problem on takeoff," I said.

"Get off me, Brandon, for cryin' out loud."

"We just crashed!" I screamed into Ricky's ear. "Hey, Ricky? Are you all right!!!?"

The kids watching thought this was great.

"Ricky! Ricky! Speak to me!" I grabbed him by the collar and shook him like a rag doll. His head bobbled back and forth. "He's dead! Call the paramedics! Call nine-one-one! Call for a pizza!"

The crowd of kids laughed like they would pee their pants. Ricky started laughing in spite of himself, but when he saw Mr. Fletcher walking toward us, he stopped laughing and started complaining loudly. "Hey, get off me. Brandon, why are you bugging me all the time? What's your problem, buddy?"

I held Ricky's face between my hands, giving him one more squeeze, which almost made his eyes pop out. "It's because I *like* you, Ricky."

Mr. Fletcher stopped in front of us.

"What's going on?"

"Ricky was in a plane crash. I saved his life," I said.

"If you came up with stuff like that in my drama class, Brandon, you might get a decent mark." Mr. Fletcher looked like he was trying not to smile.

"Mr. Fletcher, can you tell him to stop?" Ricky demanded. "Every time he sees me, he knocks me over or steps on my toe or whacks me on the head with something. Can you get him to stop? This is abuse."

"Any broken bones, Ricky?"

"No, but…"

"Cuts?

"No."

"Contusions? Concussions? Maybe a compound fracture? Bones sticking out? Lots of blood?"

"Nothing like that, but…"

"If you need protection, Ricky," said Mr. Fletcher, "you can always walk around with me." The thought of Ricky spending recess walking with a teacher for protection was hilarious. Most of the kids laughed again.

Mr. Fletcher turned to me, almost as an afterthought. "Don't knock people over, Brandon. You know the rules."

As I walked back into the school with Leon, he said quietly, "I was watching you. You've got a great act."

"What act?" I said innocently.

"Like I said, you've got a great act."

"I don't know what you're talking about," I said.

"I think you do," he said.

Chapter Nine

All of a sudden Leon changed his routine. Wednesdays and Fridays before going to work at the store, instead of going home, he rode off down Highway 2 to the east, away from town. Where was he going? I made it my business to find out.

The following Friday I skipped out of school early and hung around the gas station just outside of town on Highway 2. The kid who worked there let me pump gas while I watched the road. Leon came right on time. I could see him in the distance, but instead of passing by, he pulled into a small plaza beside the gas station and disappeared around the back. I waited a few minutes and pretended to head back to town, but I didn't see him anywhere in the plaza. I turned in to the plaza parking lot and walked along a path that led to the back of the plaza. Leon's old bicycle was leaning against the back door of a music studio. I snuck along the wall to the window and looked in. Leon had his back turned to me and was mopping the floor. He had opened the window, and I could hear guitar music. I was about to leave when a man—I guess he was the owner—came in to talk to Leon.

"When you're finished, you can clean the bathroom and the mirrors. That should be all for today."

"What time is Winnie coming?" Leon asked.

"She won't be here until about four thirty. You've got plenty of time yet."

"Okay."

"You know, Leon, pretty soon Winnie will find out."

"Find out what?" asked Leon.

"That her five dollars a week isn't enough to pay for guitar lessons. She'll see some other students paying twenty dollars and figure it out."

"Just don't tell her it's me. I want it to be a secret."

"Suit yourself." The man walked out again.

Leon continued mopping the floor. He worked carefully and then rinsed the mop out in a big sink. He took some cleaning stuff and went into another room. I walked home with new questions about Leon. He was working to help Winnie pay for her guitar lessons; that was clear. Winnie was competing in the school talent show. But why wouldn't Leon want her to know he was helping?

Winnie had become the favorite babysitter for many of the families in our building. They liked her because she was good with the kids, and she would often tidy up the place while she babysat. Most parents thought she was fourteen or fifteen, not twelve. The children always asked for her to babysit. If I happened to walk by an apartment when she was babysitting, things were happy and quiet—often happier and quieter than they were when the parents were home. Winnie was really pretty, but you could tell she was smart too. Like Leon, Winnie listened more than she spoke. Once or twice when Leon caught me watching her, he looked at me with that what-are-you-doing-looking-at-my-sister look that older brothers sometimes get. Anyone wanting to go out with her would have to get by Leon first, that's for sure.

Coming home from school one day, I saw Leon behind our apartment building. Someone had thrown out an old freezer and it was sitting, tipped on its side, next to the Dumpster. Leon was standing beside it, looking like he'd just won the lottery.

"It's still good," he said when he saw me walking over.

"What is?" I asked.

"It's still good. This freezer. The plug was wrecked, and I could feel there was a break in the cord." Leon had cut the electrical wires leading from the freezer and bared the ends of the wires. He stuck the bare ends of the wires into an extension cord he was holding. Sparks came out and the freezer began to hum. "Nothing wrong with it," he announced.

"Don't zap yourself," I said.

"So long as I don't touch both ends, I'm okay. All I need is a two-dollar plug, and we've got a good freezer."

"Why do you want a freezer?"

"To store food, genius. Here," he continued. "Help me get it to the elevator. We'll have to drag it around to the front lobby." The elevator opened in the front lobby, but it also had a big rear door that faced the loading dock at the back. People used it when they moved in or out, but it could only be opened with the superintendent's special passkey.

"Forget that," I said as I glanced around.

"Forget what?"

"Forget the front door. We'll use the moving-in door. I've got the super's key," I said, revealing one of my best-kept secrets.

"What?"

"The elevator key. I can open that back elevator door and keep it open, like when you're moving."

"You've got the elevator key?" Leon was amazed.

"One of them. I borrowed it."

"Borrowed it? When?"

"A couple of years ago. It was in the lock in the elevator. I borrowed it. When we move out, I'll give it back."

"You stole the super's key!" Leon said.

"Borrowed it. He's got another. You want my help or not?"

Leon nodded. I went to my apartment and got the key from its hiding place. I only used it late at night, when I'm not likely to be caught, like the time I put my dirt bike into the elevator to take it up to my apartment to work on.

Leon was waiting for me behind the building when I came down in the elevator and opened the rear door and stepped out. We shoved the freezer into the elevator. Once we reached his floor, we dragged it into the hall. I released the key and slipped it back into my pocket. The elevator's door closed again, and nobody knew it had been used. Together we wrestled the freezer down the fourth-floor hallway and dragged it to his door.

It was the first time Leon had ever let me into his apartment. He would usually make excuses, like "Gotta do some homework" or "It's dinnertime," when we came to the building. I would ride the smelly old elevator to the second floor, and he would go on to the fourth.

Leon's apartment was tidy, but the furniture looked old. Nothing matched. While Leon decided where to put the freezer, I had the chance to look around without being too obvious. Something didn't seem right, but I couldn't figure out what it was.

Chapter Ten

The weather stayed warm, and winter showed no sign of arriving. Our teachers talked about global warming and climate change, but we just enjoyed the good weather. Kids brought bats and balls to school and played ball during lunch. On Wednesday I saw Leon sitting in the sun, his back to the warm brick wall, and his hat pulled low over his head.

"Hey, Leon! Leon. New guy!" Toad, one of Ricky's friends, yelled. He tapped Leon's foot. Leon sat up, startled. From the look on his face, it was obvious he had been snoozing.

"Wanna play some baseball?"

Leon raised his cap, said, "No, thanks," and lowered his brim again, folding his arms as he tried to get back to sleep.

"Lots of people play baseball."

"I'm not lots of people," mumbled Leon.

"We'll let you have five strikes instead of three," Toad said.

Leon ignored him.

That afternoon in PE, the gym teacher arranged for a baseball game against the other grade eight class. If you didn't want to play, you had to sit and watch. Some kids grumbled about not being given another choice.

"How about floor hockey? We want floor hockey."

"There's only one of me and two classes. Mr. Ambrose was called to a meeting. I can't be in two places at once. Either you play ball or you watch. Take your pick," said the teacher.

We decided on a batting order, and kids in the other class took their gloves with them out into the field. Soon my class was getting skunked by Ricky's class. Ricky was pitching. He was good at it, just like he was good at everything else. Their fielders were catching everything that we batted out there. I whacked the ball as hard as I could, but they had all backed up, and the right fielder caught it near the fence. They knew I always hit deep.

Leon came to bat. Nobody knew if he could hit or not. He stood ready to bat left, and all the fielders shifted over to the right a bit. Just before Ricky pitched the ball, he crossed to the other side of the plate and cracked a deep fly ball right along the left foul line. The fielders were caught off guard and didn't get to the ball in time. Two runs came in. Leon was safe on second, but the next batter struck out and ended the inning.

Next time he was at bat, Leon stood to bat right. Ricky scowled at him and said, "Make up your mind." Leon grinned and let Ricky's first pitch go by. For the next pitch, he stood on the other side of the plate again. The fielders were more alert now. Leon popped a ball just over the first baseman, who had to run for it because the fielder, expecting another deep hit, was standing too far back.

"So you suck at basketball, but you can hit a baseball," Ricky shouted to Leon when he got to second base again.

"What happens if I hit the pitcher with a line drive?" Leon called to the gym teacher.

"Do it with intent, Leon, and you'll be on the bench."

The game ended before we had a chance to see if Leon would try to hit Ricky with a ball. Too bad. I'd been looking forward to it.

I wanted to get past Leon's front door again. I needed to take another look inside his apartment. I couldn't shake the feeling that something wasn't right. One afternoon, Leon dropped a page of his science notes as he was leaving class. He didn't notice it fall out of his binder, so I picked it up and slid it between two books of my own. Jake saw me do it, and I gave him a snitch-and-you-die look, even though I would never hurt skinny Jake.

He must have thought I was stealing Leon's work, which was fine with me. It helped my bad guy reputation.

That evening, just about suppertime, I went and knocked on Leon's door. I knew he didn't work Thursdays. Winnie answered.

"Where's Leon?" She went to get him, but she didn't invite me in. I had a chance to look inside the door. From where I stood in the doorway, I could see there were shoes on the doormat and jackets and coats in the closet. There was some weird folk music playing that sounded like something Winnie would like. I could smell spaghetti. It smelled good.

When Leon came to the door, I gave him the page of notes. "Here. You must have dropped this somewhere."

"Thanks," said Leon. He glanced at the page and turned it over. "How'd you know it was mine?" he asked.

"Lucky guess," I said.

"But it doesn't have my name on it," he said, looking at me suspiciously.

My heart went cold. I had to think fast. "But it is your handwriting, right?" I asked.

"Yeah," he answered.

"Then take it."

"Thanks," said Leon, but he gave me another funny look.

"Are you good at fixing electrical stuff?" I said, changing the subject.

"A little. Why?"

"My dirt bike. I put a new battery in and turned the key, but nothing lights up. I think there's a short somewhere."

"Let's take a look." We went to my apartment, where I showed him my dirt bike. Leon was amazed to see that it was in my bedroom. When I wasn't working on it, I hung my shirts and pants on the handlebars and foot pegs.

"Where'd you get it?" he asked.

"It was out in a field. The tires were slashed and the tank was dented, but under the seat there was a key and a manual. When I get enough cash, I'm going to get it running again."

In a few moments, Leon had found a way to unscrew a ring around the ignition switch and lift the switch away from the instrument panel. At the side of the switch were little dots of solder where wires were attached.

"See that one there? It's got a crack in it. There's your short. The red one is probably power from your battery. Gimme some pliers." Leon squeezed the dot of solder with the pliers. "Now stick the key in and turn it."

"Won't you get a shock? You're holding the key thingy," I asked.

"Can't get a shock from twelve volts," he grunted.

I turned the key, and all the lights came on.

"Let's try to start it," I suggested.

"You crazy? Your bedroom will fill with smoke."

"So?"

"You are nuts." Leon grinned as I tried the kick-starter. It didn't start, but it did pop a few times.

"Brandon! What's that noise?" my mom called from the living room.

"Nothing," I yelled back. This was great. My "dead" dirt bike was starting to come alive. Now the idea of getting it to run was not so far-fetched.

A few days later, Leon came to my place again to work on another Fletchville assignment. Because our pretend apartment was unfurnished, we had to buy furniture. We would each buy our own beds. Leon's idea was to use my mom's Sears catalog. I was going to get living room stuff and a TV because my fake income was higher than his. He was going to get a kitchen table and chairs.

When my mom let him in, I was underneath the dirt bike in my bedroom, trying to undo a stuck bolt.

"Hey," I said, waving my elbow at him, since both of my hands were busy with the bolt.

"Hey yourself," he replied, waving his elbow back at me in reply. He looked like a bird waving a wing.

I waved my elbow again. "So, what's up?"

He waved his elbow back. "Are we gonna do this homework, or what?" After that, the elbow wave became our standard greeting, sort of like a secret handshake.

We made a list of what furniture we needed for our new place. Leon said we could actually get stuff much cheaper at garage sales, but it was fun to pretend we were actually spending real money. Mr. Fletcher had given us a hint about the next assignment we would have. He warned us there would be a fire in Fletchville and somebody's apartment was going to be burned. He said we could choose whether to buy fire insurance or not, but if we chose the insurance, we had to keep a list of all our stuff and record the total cost of all of it. If we chose not to buy insurance, we had to write out our reasons why we had chosen not to. I wanted to take the easy way out and not do as much work, but Leon thought we should get the insurance. We decided to wait a few days before we made up our minds.

Leon left my place, and I guessed he was following his usual routine. There was the job at the music studio, which he did without Winnie's knowledge, and there was his regular job at the food store. Usually by ten o'clock, he would be walking home with a bag of groceries. No wonder he was always tired. Many days in class, I would see his head start to nod, and I knew that his eyes were beginning to close. A couple of times I saw his chin drop right down or his head fall to one side. Mrs. Cawfield never noticed because that was usually when somebody threw something at Roger. Roger would overreact and set the whole class in an uproar.

Chapter Eleven

"Where are you from, Leon?" Ricky asked one day when he and his buddies were standing around the school yard.

"Why?" answered Leon. "You want a postcard?"

"I just want to know, that's all," said Ricky.

"I was born in a hospital, but I don't remember much about it. The nurse was cute, that's about all... How about you?"

"I mean, where are you from? Like, what country?"

"Nova Scotia," said Leon. "It's a province, by the way." He began to walk away.

"How about before that? Jamaica? Trinidad? The States?" Ricky called after him.

Leon turned around. "Is that what you think about black people? That we're all from someplace else?"

"Well, aren't you?" asked Ricky.

Leon turned and kept walking. Ricky turned to his friends and said something. They all laughed.

The talent show was coming up soon. I behaved myself in school so I would be sure to see it. The whole school met in the gym for the show. I saw no room at the back of the gym, so I jerked my thumb at one of Ricky's friends and he moved away to let me lean on the wall with the other grade eight kids. I liked the talent shows.

Mrs. Lafferty introduced the acts. It was pretty easy to see who had practiced a lot and who hadn't. First some little kids did some kind of lip-synch act with dancing. They didn't open their mouths enough to look like real singing, and sometimes they just giggled. A girl in grade six played the piano and had to keep stopping and starting again. Another kid played a guitar. I'm no musician, but even I could tell he should have left the guitar in the case. Finally Nelson, a boy in the other grade eight class, did a stand-up comedy routine. He could keep a straight face while telling his jokes, which were on the theme of rednecks.

"You know you're a redneck when your dad walks you to school because you're both in the same grade."

"You know you're a redneck when you go to a family reunion to pick up chicks."

He started telling a rude one about an outhouse. Off at the side of the gym, Mr. Fletcher started making "cut" motions across his neck. Nelson ignored him and went on. Finally Mr. Fletcher went right up to the stage and whispered something to him.

"Just one more!" Nelson said. "How do you know if your grandma's a redneck?" he shouted. "She calls downstairs, 'Hey everybody, come on up and look at this before I flush it down!'" The kids all liked that one.

Ricky came on stage and played his guitar. He was actually pretty good. He played "Smoke on the Water" and then moved on to "Voodoo Child" by Jimi Hendrix. We all figured he had won again.

Winnie was the last one up. The performers had drawn lots, and she got picked to go last. I felt sorry for her, following Ricky, but I didn't have to feel that way for long. She came up with a guitar and a stool and then put the guitar down and stood at the microphone. She waited until the audience was quiet before she spoke.

"The song I'm going to sing is called 'Joanne Little' by Bernice Johnson Reagon." She sat down on the stool and began to play and sing. The song had a heavy beat, and when she sang it, we saw another side to Winnie. The song was tough and strong, and her face changed as she sang.

She sang well. The kids who were all cranked up because of Ricky's rock and roll act began to shut up and listen. She sometimes slapped her guitar to keep the beat. Her voice was powerful and clear. When her song ended, there was a respectful silence in the gym.

Suddenly the kids began to clap and cheer. She grinned and began another song called "In My Soul." But she suddenly got stuck. She'd play a bit and then stop. She mumbled something about being in the wrong key.

From the side of the gym where the other performers were watching, everyone heard Ricky say, "She only knows one song." There were a few giggles. Leon, who was sitting nearby, turned his head and tried to see where the giggles came from. On stage, Winnie tried some more and began to get frustrated. The whispering in the audience got louder. Again I heard Ricky say, louder this time, "She only knows one song."

Winnie finally got up and walked off the stage, her face down. Leon went out the side door to meet her in the hallway. A teacher went out to see if she was okay, and Mrs. Lafferty came up while everyone was talking about it. She thanked everyone and said the judging would be done over the lunch period, and that they would announce the winner on the PA.

The afternoon slipped by, and shortly before dismissal time, Mr. Sitzer announced on the PA that Ricky was the winner and Winnie was the runner-up. Some of us groaned. We hated to see Ricky win again.

Walking out of the school yard, I saw Ricky and his gang lounging by the fence with their skateboards. Ricky had his guitar and amp and was waiting for his mom to come pick him up. Leon was walking toward the bike racks. Everyone was wondering if Leon would do something to Ricky for insulting his sister. A crowd of kids gathered and waited to see if there would be a fight.

"Hey, Leon," called Ricky. "Leon!"

Leon walked over and stood, warily, a few meters away.

"Your sister's really pretty good," Ricky said, trying to sound sincere. We all knew he was saying that because he didn't want Leon to beat him up. Leon was bigger than Ricky and had every reason to be mad. But Leon just looked at him and at all his friends. Some had smirks on their faces. Leon looked all alone; a tall black kid with cheap clothes surrounded by a bunch of rich white kids with big allowances, fancy clothes and bad attitudes. Leon didn't say anything. He just walked over to his old bicycle and rode off. If it was me, I would have jumped Ricky and loosened a few teeth, but I guess Leon was not a fighter.

Chapter Twelve

Later that week we were finishing off our discussion of the American Revolution and the Loyalists and moving on to early Canadian settlements. "Black Loyalists were given a pretty raw deal," Mr. Fletcher said. "Coming to places like Nova Scotia, they were promised free farmland as a reward for fighting with the British. Remember, this was the land originally farmed by Acadian settlers, who had been kicked out by the same British government. When the black Loyalists got there, they were given parcels of land that were rocky or far inland, away from water sources for irrigation. The white settlers got the better land near the shores or the rivers."

"Why couldn't they just leave?" someone asked.

"In those days it cost so much to travel, most people could never afford it. Even so, where could they have gone? The United States would have jailed them for fighting for the British, and the British owned most of the country around them."

"But that's not fair," someone said.

"It certainly isn't," he answered.

"What happened to those people?"

"I'm glad you asked that. Many eventually returned to Africa. Others stayed in Nova Scotia. We have direct descendants of those black Loyalists in our school this year. Leon?"

If Leon could have turned red, he would have. He shrank a little in his seat.

"Sorry, Leon. I don't mean to embarrass you. Leon is from the Shelburne area of Nova Scotia. I saw it on his school records, and I asked him about it. It's something you should all know about."

"Why?" someone asked.

"Because we're learning about it in history."

"We're learning about Leon in history?" asked Roger, sounding clued-out. The other kids laughed.

"Your ancestors came from Nova Scotia, Leon?"

Leon nodded. "Right outside Shelburne. My mother's family had a farm there."

"This is really interesting, class," Mr. Fletcher said. "Leon George is descended from Loyalists who came to Canada long before most of our families did. His family has been in Canada for well over two hundred years. Think about that. He's more Canadian than most of us here; even Sir John A. Macdonald, our first prime minister, was born in Scotland. Leon's mother's family was here before most escaping slaves traveled the Underground Railroad from the USA. Only Native Canadians and the first settlers in Quebec have been in Canada longer. "

Leon coughed and spoke up. "Actually, Mr. Fletcher, on my dad's side, the George side, there's Native blood too."

"So that makes you twice over a Canadian with a long heritage," said Mr. Fletcher.

"That is so cool," said Cassie.

"What was your mother's ancestors' name?"

"I don't know for sure. Brindley or something," said Leon. "That was about ten generations back."

"I think, class," continued Mr. Fletcher, "if you trace your own family trees, you'll find that most of our families came to Canada in the last fifty to a hundred years. Usually from Europe and more recently from Asia and Africa. Leon might be new to Kingsville, but Leon's family certainly isn't new to Canada."

"I never knew that about you," I said to Leon after class.

"There's a lot you don't know," he answered.

After school I was walking home with Leon when Sam came running up to us.

"Leon. Leon! Can I go to Trevor's place? He's got a new game we want to try."

"Isn't Trevor the boy you were fighting with a while ago?" I asked.

"Yeah, but we're friends now. Can I go, Leon?"

Leon glanced at me. "I guess you can. I don't think Dad would mind."

"What do you mean Da—? Oh yeah. Dad." Sam looked scared all of a sudden. Then he ran off ahead.

I looked at Leon and raised one eyebrow. He didn't say anything.

A block or so ahead, we saw Sam pass some high school boys as they came in our direction. They must have said something to him, because Sam turned to look back at them, and he shouted something. One of them picked up a rock and threw it at Sam. It missed him, but even from a distance we could see the look on Sam's face. He was really mad.

Leon was off like a shot. I raced after him.

When I caught up, Leon was facing both boys, his fists ready.

"What did they say?" he demanded of Sam, who stood a little way off with tears in his eyes. "What did they say to you?" he repeated, looking at the high school boys.

"He said, 'Go home, nigger!' And then he threw a rock at me." Sam sounded defiant, but he still looked scared.

"You don't like black people?" Leon turned to the bigger of the two boys, a guy with so many piercings in his eyebrows and nose it looked like a bomb had gone off in front of him. This was a different Leon than the one who let Ricky insult his sister.

The bigger guy didn't answer but glanced at his buddy and began to walk past us. I knew he was about to do something sneaky, but I wasn't fast enough. Just as he passed Leon, he turned and punched him in the ear with a huge fist. Leon staggered, taken by surprise, and I thought he would fall. I started toward him, but he was up quickly. Like a cornered cat, he jumped on the older boy, hitting, cuffing and kneeing him. The two fell to the ground, wrestling. The second boy grabbed Leon by the shirt collar and tore it off, trying to pull him off his friend, who was now getting the worst of the fight. It was time for me to step in.

While Leon fought with fury, I was all business. Time seems to slow for me when I am fighting. Just like other people are good at chess or hockey or baseball, I am good at fighting.

The second kid let go of Leon when I hooked him in the head with my left. He turned in a rage and swung at me. I ducked his fist and waited that extra half second until he was off balance before I threw my second punch right onto his chin. That should have put his lights out, but it didn't. He reeled backward, arms spinning and when he caught his balance, he came at me again.

He was my size but a couple of years older. He didn't think like a fighter, though. He came running at me, arm and fist back, ready for a big punch. I watched it coming. I waited until he couldn't change direction, and then I ducked his fist and punched him deep in his gut. He doubled over in pain. I kneed him in the nose. His hands came up to his face, and he staggered backward. I could have hit him again, but I decided to wait and see what he would do.

"You're that Brandon kid," he mumbled as blood streamed out between his fingers. "I'll get you later," he sputtered as he stumbled away.

"Any time," I said.

Leon, meanwhile, was still wrestling with his opponent. It was ugly. Leon had managed to get on top of the other boy and started pummeling him with his fists. Leon was strong but clumsy. His hits were hard but badly aimed. Even so, all the guy was doing was trying to defend himself.

"Leon. Stop. Leave him now. He's done." I began to pull Leon off.

"Dirty bastard."

"Leon, stop. The cops will come."

"Cops? Where?" Leon looked around.

"Not yet, but let's not stick around."

"Let's get out of here. Sam, come on. We're going home." Leon's voice sounded funny. His lower lip was already swelling from a punch.

Sam had been watching the fight with wide eyes. Now, like it would for any ten-year-old, his mind jumped to what was really important to him.

"You said I could go to Trevor's!" Sam wailed. The insult and the fight were suddenly too much for him. He began to wail. "You said I could go to Trevor's. You promised."

"Those jerks live around here. I don't want them coming after you."

"You promised," cried Sam.

"That's it! I said no!"

"You promised!"

"No! You're not going." Leon was shouting.

"I am so going!"

"You go and you're grounded."

"You can't ground me!"

"Watch me."

Sam was crying uncontrollably now. He started to walk away, stumbling on the uneven ground. Leon sucked on a split knuckle and looked a bit guilty. We walked behind Sam for a few minutes, Leon looking over his shoulder every few seconds as if an army of police vehicles was on the way. The high school guys had taken off. Sam sniffled as he walked ahead of us.

Leon called out to him, "Okay. You can go over to his place. Tomorrow."

"You mean it?"

"I mean it. Don't make me change my mind," Leon said. Sam's tears dried up and he ran ahead, happy again.

Leon and I walked more slowly. I was still all pumped up. The fight hadn't lasted long enough. I was shadow-punching and ready to relive how we'd beaten those two racist creeps. I looked over at Leon and saw a tear trickle down his face.

"Hey? You hurt? Break a bone or something?"

"No."

"What's wrong, buddy? We just beat those guys. It was great. You were great."

Leon sat on a low fence that ran beside the path. "It'll never work," he said as he wiped a tear away. "I just can't do it anymore."

"Do what?" I asked. His head hung down, and he spoke so quietly I could barely hear him.

"Be the dad," Leon said.

"What?"

"Be the dad," Leon repeated.

"You mean tell Sam when he can go out and all that? If you're the oldest, your dad leaves you in charge, right? You're filling in for your dad when he's away, right?"

"No." Leon kicked at a rock. "There is no dad."

"No dad?" I asked.

"No dad."

"Then who was that guy who came with you on that first day at school?"

"He's an old friend of the family. Fred Prentice. He's an alcoholic, but he's a good guy. I paid him thirty-five dollars to drive us out here in my mom's old car and sign papers for the apartment. He stayed a few days to pretend to be our dad when we moved in."

"He's not your dad?" I was still amazed.

"My real dad died when I was six. My mom remarried a couple of years back. Last year she died too. Of cancer. She made me promise to raise Winnie and Sam the way she raised us. I've tried to do that."

"What happened to her husband? Your—what is it? Your stepdad?"

"What about him? We left." Leon kicked at another rock.

"Why did you leave?"

Leon got up again and began to walk. "Let's just say, he wasn't the great guy she thought he was. We hated him."

"Wow…" I said. "But isn't he still your stepdad?"

"Don't call him that. He's not my anything-dad."

"That bad, eh?"

Leon took a deep breath. "Don't tell anyone. Winnie never trusted him. She thought he was a creep. One night after Mom died, I caught him trying to sneak into Winnie's room when she was asleep. I grabbed him and tossed him into the hallway. I was mad enough to kill him. Instead I threatened him with the police."

"What happened then?"

"Winnie and I figured if we called the police, we would end up in some foster home with strangers… maybe we'd get split up. So we decided to move out on our own." Leon turned to look over the water. "We called Fred and asked him to help us."

"Does anyone else know you're on your own?" I asked.

"Nobody does." Leon turned to look at me. "And it has to stay that way."

"Hey. You can trust me."

"I hope so. Winnie's gonna kill me. She made me swear I wouldn't tell anyone. I made her and Sam swear too. Now I've gone and broken our first rule." Leon looked miserable.

"Tell her I guessed you were hiding something. I was trying to figure out why there are only kid-size shoes by the door and kid-style jackets in the cupboard. Today, when Sam asked you what you meant about your dad and then stopped talking? I knew he was lying. He looked like he'd swallowed a hot coal."

"He's not good at hiding anything. He doesn't think before he hits somebody or shoots off his mouth." Leon smiled.

"Anyway, I figured you were hiding something."

"Is it that easy to tell?"

"Nah. Most people wouldn't notice. Me, I like to watch what's going on, like a spy."

Leon looked at me for a long time. Another tear crept down his face, but he didn't seem to notice it.

"I get so tired," he said slowly. "Keeping the secret. Lying to people. Working, earning enough for food and rent money. Spending time with Sam, trying to keep him out of trouble…"

"So you've got no parents," I said.

"Nobody," he replied.

"No grandparents?"

"All dead."

"So how do you get by?" I asked.

"You know those 'real-life' Fletchville assignments Mr. Fletcher gives us?" said Leon, picking up another rock and throwing it into the lake. "That's how we live. We're doing Fletchville every day, me and Winnie and Sam. Go to work. Save money for the rent. Use coupons. Compare prices. Get the best deal for anything we need. Winnie babysits and tries to save money by getting a meal when she works. She'll sometimes have Sam come and eat with her. I get cheap food from the store. We don't have a computer. We do all our computer stuff at the library. We don't have cable TV. We never go to movies or do fun stuff that costs money. Does that tell you enough?"

"No. Like, who cleans up the place? Who cooks?"

"We share. But mostly Winnie and I cook. Sam does laundry and cleans the apartment." Leon wiped away another tear and stared out at the lake. "We worry all the time. We don't talk to anybody, hardly. We made up our own rules. No having anybody over to the house. No going to parties. We cancelled the phone service after registering for school. We use a pay phone to call out. If someone asks about our dad, we say he's at work. We always look through the peephole in the door before we open it. If there's a cop or someone who looks like Children's Aid, we hide until they leave."

"Cool," I said.

"You're kidding, right?" Leon sounded surprised.

"No. This is so cool."

"What's cool about it?"

"No parents. No rules. No bedtime. You can do whatever you want." I grinned at him.

Leon smiled a bit when I said this. "Come and have dinner with us" was all he said.

Chapter Thirteen

When I walked into Leon's apartment, Winnie looked from me to Leon and then gave him a What-in-the-world-are-you-doing? look.

"We're not supposed to have anyone over. You know the rules, Leon."

"It's okay."

"No, it isn't. There are *rules*, Leon."

"He knows, Winnie."

"Knows what?"

"About us."

"Leon, are you crazy?" Winnie shouted.

"I know what I'm doing," said Leon.

Winnie was furious. "We've been doing great for months now. Nobody knows, nobody even guesses."

"We had trouble today. Two kids were picking on Sam and calling him nigger. Brandon helped, big time."

"That's not a reason!"

Sam broke in. "Brandon is an awesome fighter. You should've seen him. *Bam! Bam! Bam!*" Sam made punching and kneeing motions in the air. "You were good too, Leon. But not as good as Brandon."

Leon said, "Brandon was already figuring it out on his own. It was only a matter of time." Winnie looked at me, and I could tell she was thinking I probably couldn't figure anything out on my own.

"I invited him over for dinner," continued Leon. "I'll set another place."

Winnie followed him into the kitchen, and they had a whispered conversation. It sounded a lot like cats hissing at each other. I heard only bits and pieces of it.

"He's the baddest kid in school," she snarled.

"He's a good guy." Leon sounded like he was talking through gritted teeth.

"And you trust him?"

"Yes, I trust him…"

"You might be oldest, but you're the stupidest…I'm not going to any foster home, group home or anything else just because you can't keep your mouth shut," Winnie hissed.

"…not like he seems to be…" Leon growled back.

A few minutes later, Winnie brought out spaghetti and a salad and banged it onto the table. She sat down, crossed her arms and refused to look up.

"Snap out of it, Winnie. Things will be fine." Leon was angry now.

Winnie didn't look convinced.

"Let's start," Leon said. He bent his head and closed his eyes. Winnie and Sam did too. "Oh Lord, bless this food to our use and us to your service," said Leon, "and bless Brandon and help him keep our secret. Amen." I'd never been prayed for before. It felt strange. But good.

Their dishes and cutlery were old but clean. Some of it matched. Everyone helped themselves from the pot on the table. I was surprised that, here at home, Sam had good manners. He said "please" and "thank-you" and it was natural, not like he was putting it on. So he wasn't always the angry noisy kid I saw at school. After supper they cleaned up. Everyone did something different. Sam washed the dishes. Winnie dried, handing back to Sam any dishes with spots on them. Leon cleaned and wiped the table, put away the food and put the clean dishes in the cupboards.

After supper, Sam wanted to watch some wrestling show that he liked, but Leon said, "Homework first." He sounded like my mom.

"Come on, Leon. I never get to see wrestling. Everyone is talking about it. And it's on one of the channels we get."

"Homework first. We don't want Mrs. Grace trying to contact our 'dad' about missing work."

"Aw, Leon…" Sam seemed his old self again.

"Sam!" Leon raised his voice a bit. Sam grumbled and went to the bedroom to do his spelling and math.

"See, Brandon? We have rules. So it isn't all 'cool.' I can't wait until I'm older and can do this legally and not have to lie to people all the time."

"You can't help being the adult. It's okay to lie if it's for something good."

Leon looked serious. "No, it's not okay to lie. It's just that I don't know what else to do right now. But do me a favor. Don't mention our fight to anybody. No bragging. I mean, I'm glad we whipped their butts, but I don't want anyone knowing about it."

"But it would help you. People like Ricky would think twice about insulting you or your family."

"Ricky's trouble no matter what happens. Just don't say anything, okay? I don't want people asking questions about us or noticing us in any way."

"You don't want people noticing you?" I asked.

"No way," Leon said.

"Then why'd you come to Kingsville?"

"What do you mean?" he asked.

"You're the only black family in a town of white people. You guys stand out like licorice on a snow cone."

Leon laughed suddenly. "Yeah, that was a mistake. I picked this town because it was the closest place to Toronto we could afford."

At school, Winnie didn't smile anymore when she saw me coming. In fact she avoided looking at me, almost as if she thought I would blurt out their secret to somebody. Leon was quieter too. We had another Fletchville assignment to do—find an ad for a used car and fill out the sheet Fletcher gave us to help calculate the down payment and interest and all that stuff—but when I suggested to Leon we could work on it together, he claimed he had to work extra shifts all week. I was disappointed. It was unlike me to want to do homework, but I still wasn't ready to be working on my own.

I started worrying about Leon and his family. Now that I knew about their situation, I kept an eye on their place and made sure I walked by an extra time every evening. I strolled down their hallway, half expecting the Children's Aid to come storming along with a bunch of cops. But after a week or two, nothing happened. That made sense. I was the only one Leon had told. As far as I was concerned, nobody would get their secret from me.

After a while, Winnie and Leon seemed to relax more around me, and things seemed to go back to normal. I could go and visit their place from time to time and not be left standing at the door.

Chapter fourteen

It was Leon who saw the body first. We were walking along the deserted lakefront by the beach, letting the wind blow in our faces. I liked the fishy smell of the water, the freshness of it.

"Hey, look." Leon pointed to something about three waves out from the rocky shore. It came in and out with the water, not floating but rolling. I couldn't tell what it was. It looked like a big brown carpet somebody had dumped in the water. Now and then, a small gray circle of stringy stuff, like a halo, would float from one end.

I walked closer to Leon, and I could see that the gray stuff was hair. Below the hair was the pale gray skin of a dead face. Its eyes and mouth were open. There was gray stubble on the chin and cheeks. I jumped back.

Leon was one of those people who don't freak out when he sees a dead body. In fact, he started wading into the cold water for a better look. It looked like he was thinking about trying to pull the body out. No rescue was needed here, though. I could tell this old guy was dead. Real dead.

Of course, having to maintain appearances, I stayed where I was and let the skin crawl back and forth across the back of my neck while Leon waded to shore. I didn't want him knowing that seeing a real live dead guy was enough to make me yark all over the pebbles.

"We have to tell someone," said Leon.

I was still staring in horror at the body rolling in and out. Maybe someone killed him right here, I thought. Maybe that person is watching us. The hair stood up on my neck.

"You can't leave bodies in the water without telling anybody. We have to report it." Leon made it sound like he was always finding dead bodies lying around.

"Let's get out of here. Let somebody else report it."

"Hey, his family is probably searching for him. This guy needs a proper burial."

"I don't think he needs anything," I said.

"Maybe he was someone's granddad." Leon looked around. I could tell what he was thinking. Adults ask questions. Reporters would come. And police. He couldn't talk to police. The body kept rolling in and out. It wasn't about to go anywhere. Across Lakeshore Road was a small plaza with a pay phone.

"You call," he said to me.

"No way. Leave him. Let's go," I said. I was getting very creeped out.

"Wimp." Leon snorted and walked across the street to the plaza. I followed. When Leon called 9-1-1 he tried to make his voice sound deeper. I could hear the 9-1-1 operator through the earpiece.

"Hello, nine-one-one. Would you like fire, police or ambulance?"

"I found a body. A drowned man."

"I'm transferring this call to the ambulance and police. Where is the victim now? Is he or she breathing?"

"This guy is dead. Real dead. Rolling around in the water just opposite the plaza on Lakeshore Drive in Kingsville."

"What is your name and address please?"

"I don't want to get involved." I could see Leon thinking up an excuse. "I was grounded by my dad and I'm not supposed to be out."

"Is this a prank call? It is against the law to make a prank call."

"Just tell the police to look for the body," Leon said before he hung up. I was impressed. He was pretty smooth.

Ten minutes later we were watching the action on the beach from the balcony of his apartment.

"Whatcha looking at, Leon?" Sam came and stood on the bottom rail of the balcony to see what we were staring at.

"See those cops and that ambulance?"

"Yeah."

"Well, there's a body in the water, and they just pulled it out."

"Cool! How do you know?" Sam looked at him doubtfully.

"Because I saw it and called them."

"What did it look like?" Sam's eyes were huge. This was big stuff for a ten-year-old.

"Well…he was an old white guy, kind of a gray face. A dark brown coat. He looked pretty dead."

"Did you touch it?"

"No. It was too far out to pull in."

"Were you scared?"

"A little." Leon laughed. "And Brandon was petrified."

"Winnie! Winnie! Leon found a body! And Brandon was petrified." Sam ran inside to tell Winnie, who was folding laundry in front of the TV.

"Now don't start telling everybody I saw the body," Leon warned me. "The last thing we need is the cops asking a bunch of questions."

"What's Sam talking about? What body?" Winnie asked. "Are the police going to come here?"

"No," Leon replied. "I'm not stupid. I made an anonymous call."

"I'm going down there!" said Sam.

"NO!" Winnie and Leon yelled together.

"Don't go down there," Leon added. "I mean it."

"I can't have any fun," said Sam. "*You* get to see bodies and stuff."

"So, become an undertaker. You'll see lots of bodies then," Leon replied.

It was only about an hour before the police pulled up in front of our apartment building. Someone at the plaza must have seen Leon use the phone, and finding the address of the only black teenager in Kingsville hadn't been too much for our local cops to handle.

We watched from the balcony as a policeman got out of the car and walked into the lobby of our building. Leon, Winnie and Sam looked nervous.

"You idiot!" Winnie said to Leon. "What are we going to do?"

"Into the bedroom. Don't make a sound. Don't answer the door," Leon ordered.

We huddled on Leon's bed in the small bedroom he shared with Sam and listened to a large hand knock repeatedly on the door. Winnie shook every time she heard a knock. "Serves you right, phoning nine-one-one," she hissed angrily. "They'll just keep coming back."

Leon looked scared too, but he attempted to reassure her. "Yeah, and we won't answer. They'll get tired of it.

If they come to the school, let me talk to them. Don't you guys say anything."

"We don't know anything anyway," Sam whispered. "I only wish I'd seen the body."

The police came twice more to our building, but Leon and his family never answered the door. Leon said he couldn't add anything to their investigation anyway.

A week later the newspaper reported that the drowning victim had gone missing from an old-age home. An anonymous caller had reported the body in the water. The death was ruled an accident, and the police closed the investigation. Leon seemed to relax a bit after that, but they still never opened their door to strangers.

Chapter Fifteen

Even though he had to earn money, pay bills and lie to just about everyone, Leon seemed to be pretty cool about it all. But all that changed one November afternoon. Leon knocked on my apartment door. "Have you seen Sam?" he asked. I hadn't. I stepped into the hall and closed my door so my parents couldn't hear us.

Leon looked scared. Sam had not come home after school. The unbreakable rule was that Sam had to come home from school before he did anything else. He was two hours late. Leon didn't look cool. He looked worried.

"You want me to help find him?" I asked.

"Yeah. And I don't want anyone else to know."

I made an excuse to my mother and went out with Leon. He had phoned one or two of Sam's friends from the pay phone already, but they hadn't seen him.

"If he's run away, it'll ruin everything. Children's Aid will find out."

"Why would he run away?"

"Maybe 'cause of yesterday. He didn't clean the place, and I yelled at him. He said he was just a kid and he was sick of having to do everything. I told him he wasn't old enough to go out and work in a grocery store, so he had to help at home. I think he misses Mom. He's not old enough to be without parents."

"Sam never stays mad long. Maybe he's lost," I suggested.

"How can you get lost in this town? It's too small."

"Not to a ten-year-old, it isn't," I said.

In the end we split up to look around. I decided to think like a ten-year-old and search the places where a kid his age could go and lose track of time. I headed to the industrial park outside of town where I used to skateboard on the cement truck ramps and loading docks. No Sam.

I remembered other things I had done when I was ten. I used to climb the roofs in the industrial park. At a sandblasting factory I saw a discarded shoe lying at the bottom of a pipe that ran up the side of the building. The shoe looked to be about the same size as Sam's. I'd known kids to climb up on a roof and then be too afraid to climb down again.

I grabbed the pipe with both hands and climbed, my feet scrabbling up the wall. I was almost to the top of the building when I slipped. My feet lost their grip and slid down the wall. With a sound like the crack of a gun, my head hit the steel siding and I saw a burst of white stars. I hung on to the pipe with all my strength. Below me was a long fall and broken bones. My feet bicycled against the wall and began to grip again, and I was able to pull myself up. Blood dripped from my eyebrow and down my face. No chance to wipe it away. I could see drops of it hitting the ground below me.

A noise came from inside the building, and an outside door banged open. Someone was coming out to see what the noise was. I climbed up the remaining five feet and swung myself over the top of the wall, rolling onto the pea stones on the roof, hoping whoever was down there wouldn't see the blood.

Panting with the effort, I lay still for a few minutes. While I lay there, I looked across the flat roof in the growing twilight. No Sam. I had climbed all that way for nothing. I waited until I heard the door bang shut before I climbed down.

Another factory roof was easier to climb. It had a ladder that started about ten feet up. All I had to do was balance on the edge of the recycling bin and reach up to it. Sam could probably have done it too, but he wasn't on that roof either.

Behind the sawmill was a huge pile of sawdust and a tower that looked like a short fat rocket. My dad had told me it was a dust collector, like a big vacuum cleaner for sawdust. It had a ladder that reached the ground, but the company had installed a security camera on it. Behind the security camera was a pile of scrap lumber. I picked up a long piece of board, snuck up behind the camera and covered the security camera's lens with the board. I felt like I was in a spy movie. But when I got to the top of the dust collector, there was no Sam. Just sawdust and bird droppings.

I returned to Leon's apartment, hoping Sam had come back on his own, but one look at Leon's face showed he hadn't. Winnie was staring out from their balcony.

"It's past six. He's never that late." Winnie noticed my bloodstained eyebrow and shirt. "What happened to you, Brandon? Come here and let me clean you up." She took me by the hand and led me to the bathroom sink. It was a clean bathroom with three toothbrushes lined up neatly in a holder.

"You need another toothbrush," I said as Winnie gently cleaned my face with a warm washcloth. It felt nice having her wash my face. Up close she was even prettier.

"What do you mean?"

"You need a fourth toothbrush. And a pair of men's shoes for your front closet. If anyone ever does come in here, they'll know right away you don't have a dad here."

"You notice a lot," she said quietly. Leon went to the pay phone and told his boss he'd be late for work. Winnie had no way out of her babysitting job for that night, so she took her homework with her and told us to let her know as soon as we found Sam. She left a note on the door for Sam, in case he turned up.

Leon and I went to the town bus depot, which was in the back of the pizza place. Leon asked the clerk if his brother had bought a bus ticket, but she hadn't seen him. She told us they wouldn't sell a ticket to a kid anyway. After we left, Leon decided he didn't want to risk asking anyone else if they'd seen Sam.

We searched along the shore in the darkness. Now and then Leon would stop and hurl a rock into the water. "Suppose some weirdo has kidnapped Sam," he said. "Where *is* that kid?"

We were about to turn for home when I remembered something. "Come with me," I said. I led Leon away from the shoreline and back toward the railroad tracks. The tracks were deserted, and in the darkness it was hard to find the dirt path that led eastward, but I managed to follow it.

"Where are we going? There's nothing here," Leon said.

"Just an idea. Something I used to do." We walked a few hundred meters, and then I turned right onto an even smaller shortcut that led across the train tracks to the next street. There was a small cement drainage pipe leading under the tracks. One end of it was beside the path, barely visible except as a black circle in the dark. Leon walked beside me, muttering that there was nothing here at all.

"Sam!" I shouted into the pipe.

"Help me!" A small voice came from deep inside the pipe. "I'm stuck! Help me!"

"Where is he? What's he doing?" Leon shouted at me.

"It's a drainage pipe. I used to crawl in there to hear the freight trains pass by over my head."

"Sam! It's me, Leon." Leon was shouting like a wild man.

"I can't get out, Leon. I'm stuck."

"How'd you get in there?" Leon yelled.

"I crawled in."

"Why?"

"To hear the trains!"

"See? I told you," I said to Leon.

"You can't move?"

"No. I'm stuck." Sam's voice sounded hollow and far away.

"Can you breathe?"

"Yeah. But I'm real cold."

Leon tried to get into the pipe, but his shoulders were too wide. "You try," he demanded, but I couldn't fit in either. The cement pipe grated against my shoulders and back as I tried to squeeze in. All was blackness. Sam was impossible to see.

"I can't fit either. I'm way too big now."

"I'll call the fire department to get you out," Leon shouted to Sam.

"They'll find out about us, Leon," wailed Sam. "They'll send us to a foster home."

"We can't leave you there, Sam. We need help to get you out."

Leon must have been desperate to be willing to risk their secret life.

"You don't have to call the cops, Leon. We can get him out without anyone knowing. Trust me."

Leon looked hopelessly at me.

"Sam, it's me, Brandon," I called into the pipe. "I almost got stuck in there once. You're gonna be okay. How'd you get stuck, Sam?

Sam's answer came as a breathless stream of words. "I crawled in to hear the train and I waited and I got scared because it was too tight and I crawled farther ahead to get out and it got narrow and now I can't go forward and I can't go back."

"Are your arms behind you or in front of you?"

"What?"

"Are your arms stretched out in front of you or lying behind you?"

"No."

"No what?"

"My arms are bent. My elbows are against the pipe and my hands are near my face."

"That's not so good," I whispered to Leon. "But maybe we can still get him out."

"I'm sorry, Leon," called Sam. "I should have come home from school, but the kids said this was fun."

"Listen, Sam. We're going to get you out of there.

Just be calm." Leon looked worried. "We should call the police," he said to me.

"I think Winnie could fit in there," I said. "She could pull him back."

"Then I'll have my whole family stuck in the pipe," Leon said angrily.

"Give me twenty minutes. If I can't get him out, you can call the SWAT team or fire department or whoever you want, but give me a chance first." I ran to our apartment building to get Winnie while Leon stayed with Sam.

Winnie had just finished babysitting, and she had a hard time believing me when I told her where Sam was. But I had a plan. I asked Winnie to fill a bucket with warm water and bring a bottle of dish soap and a flashlight. We went back as fast as we could manage without spilling the water.

Leon and Winnie began arguing about how to get Sam out, while I shone the flashlight into the drainage pipe. I could see Sam jammed in near the far end.

"Shut up. You'll scare him," I said. "Sam?" I called. "We're going to pour soapy water into the pipe, and Winnie is going to crawl in and pull you back out the way you came in."

"Why get me all wet?" came Sam's hollow voice.

"We need to make you slippery."

Winnie fit in the pipe, but just barely. We poured water into the pipe but it poured back out again. "We have to pour from the other side. It's sloping this way,"

I told them. Leon and I crossed the tracks to where the pipe was open on the other side. Into the pipe went the soapy water.

"Leon, I'm getting all wet," wailed Sam.

"That's good," said Leon. "We'll get you dry soon."

We could hear Winnie crawling in from the other side. Her voice was hollow, like Sam's.

"How did you get in here, Sam? It stinks!"

After a few minutes, Sam said he could wiggle his arms a bit because of the soapy water.

"Can you feel me? I'm touching something—is it you, Sam?" called Winnie from inside the pipe.

"That's my foot, Winnie. Pull me out!" Sam sounded desperate. We listened to the grunts and struggles from both of them as Sam was pulled back through the narrow concrete pipe. Leon and I were on the other side again, watching as first Winnie's feet and legs appeared, twisting like a rumba dancer. Her coat and arms were soaked with water as she emerged and leaned down to pull her brother the rest of the way out.

"Thank God you're safe. Thank God…" Leon said over and over as he hugged them both. I stood apart in the darkness beside the railroad tracks. A single street-light illuminated the relief and joy on their faces.

The four of us slowly walked home, Sam still sobbing with relief and shivering at the same time.

"It was so dark and I was so cold and I had to pee and I couldn't wait."

"So that's what that smell was," said Winnie, laughing.

"I thought I would die in there, I really did. I called and called, but nobody could hear me."

"It must have been awful," said Leon sympathetically. "You were in there a long time."

"How did you find me?"

"Brandon figured it out," said Leon. "I thought he was nuts, coming to this place in the dark." All three of them looked at me, and Leon added, "But he was right. I was ready to call the fire department and the police and everything. I was ready to blow our cover to get you out. But Brandon was right again. He said we could get you out without everyone finding out about us."

"You were right to trust Brandon. He's cool," said Winnie, walking beside me. She smiled at me, and I felt an achy feeling right down to my toenails. When we got to their place, Winnie got cleaned up and changed into warm clothes. Sam was shivering so badly, Leon made him take a bath to get warmed up.

After Sam was finally settled on the old couch with a mug of hot chocolate, Leon saw me to the door. "Thanks," he said quietly as I left.

Chapter Sixteen

Christmas was coming. The snow came late and not much fell, but the stores were full of Christmas stuff and the streetlamps had strings of lights all over them. Tinny Christmas music came over speakers in the downtown area, and at the band shell a Santa Claus came to give presents to little kids, courtesy of the Downtown Business Improvement Association.

Leon seemed to be working more and more, and I didn't see much of him. Sam got a paper route and began delivering papers in our building and on the streets nearby. He looked like a miniature Leon, walking fast and coming home in the darkness. At school I didn't see him in the office as often. He was probably too tired to get in trouble.

Every year during the last week of classes before Christmas, we had an assembly for the first ten minutes of each morning. Mrs. Lafferty hosted it. She played the piano, and all the kids sang Christmas songs, reading the words from the overhead projector.

On Monday, Tuesday and Wednesday we sang the usual songs for ten minutes and then were dismissed to our classes. Most of the older kids slouched along the back wall and let the little kids do all the singing. On Thursday we warmed up with a few traditional songs. Then a girl named Mariessa played the piano. She played well too; something by Bach, she said. But the biggest surprise was when Winnie got up, went to the front of the audience and got her guitar and a stool from behind the stage curtains. She had a determined look on her face as she set the stool down. Some kids looked at Ricky, waiting for him to say something nasty.

A girl named Alyson joined her, and Winnie announced they would sing "Silent Night" as a duet. Winnie told the history of the song, how it was first composed for guitar because an old organ in some little German town had broken down. The two girls sang well together, with Alyson singing the melody and Winnie harmonizing. The audience applauded, and some of the kids whistled through their teeth. Winnie remained standing. She glanced at Ricky and announced, "I've got another song prepared." Ricky said something to his friends, and they all laughed.

Winnie introduced the song as a hymn that came from a remote place called Appalachia. Nobody ever found out who composed it, she told us. A musician heard a little girl singing it and paid her five dollars to keep singing until he had written it out. It was called "I Wonder as I Wander." Winnie strummed the guitar and began to sing. None of us had heard the song before, but everyone seemed to like it. It wasn't like a regular Christmas carol. It was more like the blues. Winnie's sweet voice filled the whole gym. The kids stopped talking and listened.

> *I wonder as I wander out under the sky,*
> *How Jesus, the Savior, did come for to die,*
> *For poor ordn'ry people like you and like I.*
> *I wonder as I wander...out under the sky...*

She sang three more verses to a completely silent gymnasium. The words were simple but they felt real to me. One of the teachers wiped tears from her eyes. Winnie stopped singing and stood with her head down. Then she smiled as everyone clapped and cheered. She bowed once and then sat down. Leon grinned and shot a look at Ricky, as if daring him to make some rude comment.

As the Christmas holidays got closer, nobody felt like working. On Thursday a fierce north wind was blowing snow in our faces when we went outside after lunch. We huddled in a big group outside the side door of the school to try to keep warm. Leon stood nearby dressed in his out-of-style ski jacket, which looked too thin for the weather. Ricky's buddies gathered close, hiding Ricky and one of his friends, who had cigarettes going. Ricky began to make up a song about smoking.

> *I've got the emphysema blues,*
> *I'm sick from my knees to my shoes.*
> *This smoking's as bad as they said,*
> *In a few more minutes I'll probably be dead.*

Everybody laughed, even Leon, and we all stopped talking to hear if Ricky could make up any more verses.

"What rhymes with cancer?" he asked.

A few kids made suggestions: "Prancer." "Chance-her." "Answer." "Enhancer."

> *Well, these smokes are givin' me cancer,*
> *And I know it ain't the answer.*
> *And I'm at the end of my blues song…*
> *'Cause the only black brother won't sing along…*

The crowd looked at Leon to see what he would do.

Leon grinned. "Keep smoking," he said. "It will give you one of those raspy voices like those old blues singers who drink and smoke too much."

"Ooooh…Clean up in aisle seven," Ricky smirked.

"At least I earn my own money," answered Leon, turning away.

Oooo Eeee Oooo I've got the grocery story bluesssss
There's a milk spill in aisle seven and I'm wettin' my
   shooooesssss
My boss only pays me seven bucks an hour—

Ricky paused and took a drag from his smoke.

—And when I get home I stink of veggies and cat food
   so I need a hot shower…

Most of the kids laughed again. Leon looked at his shoes. I felt sorry for him. Like the rest of us, he was no match for Ricky's wit.

fresh snow fell heavily that night. I loved the *crumping* sound it made under my feet as I was walking my rounds. The streets were deserted until an old car did a four-wheel drift around a corner. Ricky's brother, Mike, was driving, with Ricky and two of his friends in the car. The wheels spun furiously, and the car fishtailed back and forth while all the guys inside laughed. They turned in to the parking lot in front of the grocery store and started to do donuts. Then they stopped and got out of the car. Their voices carried clearly in the cold night air. One of Ricky's friends, a guy they called Toad, crouched behind the middle of the rear bumper and held on to it.

"We'll take it slow. Pound on the trunk if we're going too fast," said Mike.

"Okay." Toad sounded doubtful. The others got back in, and Mike started driving through the parking lot while Toad hung on the back, sliding on his boots in the new snow. The other kids had the windows open, ignoring the cold air, shouting encouragement. Mike went faster, and I could see Toad trying to bang the trunk lid, but he couldn't let go long enough to do it.

"Hang on, Toad! Yeeee-haaaa! Ride 'em cowboy," Ricky yelled. The rest of the guys were laughing as Mike steered toward a pile of old snow between the parking lanes. The old car smashed through the snowbank, and Toad lost his grip on the bumper and flew through the air a meter or two before landing in the snow. The car stopped again and they all got out, laughing at him.

"Let's do it again," shouted Ricky.

"*You* do it. I don't think I want to," groaned Toad.

"No. We'll take it easy on you this time. Promise. No going through snowbanks, right, Mike?"

"Yeah, sure," said Mike, and they climbed back in the car. Mike slowly accelerated the car while Toad, crouching, held on. After a few gentle circles, Mike again steered for the snowbank and this time hit it even faster, sending Toad spinning through the air before he landed spread-eagled on the snowy parking lot.

"Hey, you guys said you wouldn't…" I could hear Toad complaining above the hoots and laughter.

I was about to walk on when Leon came out of the grocery store with a box of groceries. He was walking across the parking lot when Ricky spotted him.

"Hey, Leon!"

Leon ignored him.

"Hey! Hey, you deaf? Want a ride?"

"No thanks," said Leon. They came closer to him.

"Come on. It's just a short ride," said Ricky. "Here, we'll even help you with your groceries."

"I said no thanks."

"You can ride the bumper like Toad here. That way you don't have to be in the car with us."

"You've all been drinking. I'm not stupid enough to get in a car with you."

"You calling us stupid for getting in a car with ourselves?" Ricky asked and then shouted to his friends, "Hey, should I be in the car with myself? I think he's insulting us."

Leon hoisted his grocery box a little higher and began walking away.

"Hey! Hey, Leon! Your sister is hot!"

Leon stopped walking and stood there, his back still turned to them.

"Yeah, she told me she wants me too." Ricky paused. "She likes white meat, and I like dark meat. I'm not prejudiced."

Leon deliberately set his box down in the snow and walked slowly back toward the group of boys. His fists were balled at his sides, and I knew he was about to lose it.

I began to run toward them, slipping and sliding on the snow. I knew that Mike was a dirty fighter. He could be counted on to go two-on-one if he thought nobody would stop him. Leon stood facing Ricky and his brother; the two others stood close beside him. I came running up and slid into the group of them, causing two of them to fall like bowling pins.

"Brandon. What're you doing here?" Ricky asked. "Escort service?" He laughed. I could tell he'd been drinking. No wonder he was so brave.

"Fair fight," I said.

"Who said anything about a fight?" slurred Ricky. "I was telling Leon what a hot sister he has."

"Fair fight," I said again. "One-on-one."

"My sister doesn't like white trash. Neither do I," Leon said.

"Who are you calling trash?" Ricky stepped forward and without warning sucker-punched Leon in the mouth. Leon fell back and struggled up again. He approached Ricky slowly, with one fist dropped low and the other one ready. This time when Ricky tried to hit him, Leon ducked and connected with Ricky's cheek.

The blow knocked Ricky over. He glanced at his older brother. Mike was about my size, but even though he was older, I knew he was afraid of me.

"You step in there, you die," I warned him. Mike smiled a little and put his hands in his pockets. He stood watching his brother and Leon circle each other. Ricky tried to kick, but Leon caught his foot and lifted it, causing Ricky to lose his balance and fall on his back. Ricky got up again and came forward with fists ready. Leon waited and let Ricky make the first move. *He's learning*! I thought. This wasn't the wild Leon I had seen before. He was smarter tonight. More in control. Ricky came closer, seeming a little off balance, and swung widely at Leon. Leon ducked and cracked his elbow into Ricky's mouth. Beside me, Mike started forward to jump on Leon, but I grabbed his expensive coat and shoved him back. I was looking for an excuse to lay a beating on Mike, and he knew it. Suddenly Ricky held his hands forward, palms up. Blood was smeared around his mouth. "Okay. Just kidding."

Leon breathed noisily as he struggled to regain his breath. He stood, fists ready, waiting for Ricky to try some new trick.

"Serious. I don't want to fight." Ricky's voice was slurred. "Just messing around."

"Stay away from my sister." Leon glared at Ricky and stood where he was until the four of them got back in their car and drove away into the night.

"Thanks again, Brandon," Leon said quietly, picking up his box of groceries.

Chapter Seventeen

Ricky's black eye was the subject of much conversation at school the next day. "You should see the other guy," he said. "He's beat black all over." Few people guessed he meant Leon. Leon didn't say anything about it, but he had the satisfaction of seeing how Ricky kept out of his way. Leon wouldn't let me tell anyone he had beaten Ricky. Out of respect for his wishes, I didn't.

School ended for the Christmas break, and everybody went home in a happy mood. A few days later my mom offered to drive me to the mall in Springfield to do some Christmas shopping. I went to Leon's apartment to see if they wanted to come. I waved my elbow, and Leon barely even looked up. He was sitting on the couch, and Winnie was staring out the balcony window.

"Want to come Christmas shopping at the Springfield Mall? I'm getting a ride with my mom."

"We can't," said Leon.

"Who says? You can do what you want."

"Tell him," said Winnie.

"I've lost my job. We have no money to spend at the mall."

"Lost your job?" I was amazed. "What happened?"

"Ricky's mom."

"What?"

Leon explained how it had happened. The night before, Ricky's mom had come into the grocery store where Leon worked. She asked the manager if her Ricky could get a job there, and the answer was "Not until he is fourteen."

"But you've got a thirteen-year-old working here now," she said. "Why does he get to work when my Ricky can't?"

The manager insisted that no thirteen-year-old worked there. "Company policy," he said. Ricky's mom told him that Leon George was only thirteen. The manager confronted Leon when he came in to work, and Leon admitted he had lied about his age. The manager was sorry, but he told Leon he had to go. "Company policy," the manager said. "As soon as you turn fourteen, you can come back."

"That won't be until May! I need the money now," begged Leon. The manager didn't budge.

Leon finished the story and stood looking out the window with his hands in his pockets.

"We have maybe two hundred and thirty-five dollars under my bed, and rent is due next week. Rent is three hundred," Leon continued.

"I can make forty dollars in two weeks," offered Sam.

"Thanks, buddy, but you can't make sixty-five in one week. Besides, we have to eat too. What are we going to do without all that free food I bring home from the store?"

"I'll babysit more," said Winnie.

"There's only so many families in our building."

"We can sell the TV," suggested Sam with a shudder.

"We found it in the garbage. Nobody would pay much for it."

"We can try. Maybe we'd get twenty-five bucks."

"And then what?" said Leon. "What do we sell then? Our mix-and-match furniture? Our garage-sale pots and pans and dishes?" Leon went to the closet and put on his coat. "I'm going out for a while. Save supper for me," he said to Winnie.

When I looked out my balcony window later on that evening, Leon was at a house down the street, shovelling someone's driveway.

"I need to make some money," I announced to my dad. "Can I wash your truck?"

"It's freezing cold out, Brandon. You can't wash it in this weather." He and my mother exchanged glances. "Are you in trouble?" he added.

"No. I just want to make some money."

"You know…people will expect you to do as you're told…" Dad and Mom grinned at each other.

"Yeah, I figured that would be part of it."

"And you still want to work?"

"Yeah."

"John Wong at the GOOF needs a dishwasher. Why not try him?"

The GOOF was a Chinese restaurant in town. The neon sign was supposed to read:

G O O D F

O

O

D

But the top D had burned out years ago, so everyone called the place the GOOF.

When I got in the door, I didn't know what to say.

A waitress smiled at me. "Take out?"

"No. I want to work. I mean, a job. I mean, who do I talk to?"

"I get manager," she said. A small Asian man in a white apron came out of the kitchen, drying his hands as he walked.

"Yes?"

"I want a job washing dishes."

"Who tell you I need dishwasher? How you know that?"

"My dad, Stan Clifford, he told…"

"Big Stan? He your dad?"

"Yes."

"He my friend. You work hard?"

"Pardon?"

"You can work hard? Hard worker?"

"Yes, I am a hard worker," I lied. I'd never tried to work hard before, but now seemed a good time to learn.

He told me to come back Friday afternoon at four o'clock sharp. "Not late," he added.

"Four o'clock sharp," I said.

My job at the GOOF consisted of dodging hot steam coming out of a huge square dishwasher I called Phil. Phil had a big mouth where I slid in a green plastic tray full of dirty dishes. Then I closed a big steel door to keep the water in. I pressed a button, and Phil did the rest. That part was easy, but then I had to unload the clean dishes from the other end. At first they were too hot to touch. I stacked the bowls and plates and put the burning hot knives and forks and spoons into separate sections on another plastic tray so I could bring them back out. The dishes and cutlery were so hot they steam-dried within a half minute or so—no spots. All the dirty dishes had to be rinsed first with a big sprayer that hung down over the sink. It was powerful enough to shoot water across the room. I was tempted to hose the waitresses down when things got dull, but I didn't. This wasn't school.

I kept my job a secret from Leon. I wasn't sure if he would understand why his friend took the only available part-time job in Kingsville.

A few nights later, when I was visiting Leon and Winnie and Sam, there was a brief knock and an envelope came sliding under the door. Then there was silence.

"What's that?" asked Leon.

Sam went to see. "It's an envelope. No address."

"What's inside it?" asked Winnie.

"Money," said Sam. He counted out some bills slowly. His eyes lit up. "Forty dollars," he announced.

"What else is in it?" Leon wanted to know.

"Nothing. Just the money."

Leon looked at me. "What's going on?"

"Don't ask me," I said.

"Maybe it's a Christmas gift," Winnie suggested.

"Why wouldn't somebody put a card in then?" asked Leon.

"Maybe it's from one of Winnie's families. They all think she's great," I said.

"I'm not forty dollars worth of great. When they want to tip me, they give it to me when they come home," answered Winnie.

Leon looked doubtful. "Nobody knows we need money. Nobody knows I got fired except my boss, us and you. Who did you tell?"

"Nobody," I replied truthfully.

"Who did you tell?" Leon repeated. "Who knows about us?"

"Nobody!" I insisted.

Winnie came to my defense. "He said he didn't tell! Brandon's our friend."

"So why would somebody slip money under the door? I don't want handouts." Leon looked bewildered.

"What do you want to do with it then, stupid? Leave it in the hallway?" Winnie asked.

"Well, we can't keep it!" Leon replied.

"Sure we can keep it. Maybe somebody feels sorry for us since our 'dad' seems to disappear a lot. And it's Christmas." Winnie paused and turned to face Leon. "Are you too proud to accept help?"

"Of course not." Leon looked thoughtful and turned to his brother. "What do you think we should do with the money, Sam?"

"Keep it. I don't want to go to no foster home."

Leon turned to me. "What do you think, Brandon?"

"Keep it. Someone figures you need the money."

Leon gave me a funny look.

Sam said, "I'll settle this." He walked over to Leon, took the envelope from him and brought it to Winnie. "Put it with the rest of the money," he said to her.

Chapter Eighteen

On Christmas Eve, my parents and I dressed up and went to the candlelight service at the local church. We went because my mother insisted. We sometimes went at Easter too. My dad would put on a tie and slip the knot up to the place where his top button wouldn't close. His suit had wide lapels, and he told me that's because he'd bought it for a friend's wedding in the seventies. He didn't wear suits any other time.

The seats were hard, but the candles smelled nice. Halfway through counting the dangling lights, I noticed Leon, Winnie and Sam slipping into seats at the back. What were they doing here? Winnie saw me looking and gave me a wink. I looked away. I didn't know if it was a rule, but winking was probably wrong in a church. Unlike school, where anything goes, I usually behaved at church. I didn't want God to give me a swat or send a bolt of lightning to fry my behind. We listened to the choir and the sermon and sang a few Christmas hymns. I yawned a lot. Finally it was over.

"You come here every Sunday?" I asked Leon as we shuffled out the back after the last hymn.

"No. They would ask questions," Leon whispered.

"So why do you come now?"

"Lots of folks come only for Christmas. We won't be noticed tonight."

"Why do you come at all? Like, my parents make me, but nobody is telling you to."

"Mom wanted me to raise these two right." He jerked his thumb at Winnie and Sam. "She always wanted us to go to church, so I do it out of respect for her."

"I'd be mad at God if I were you," I said.

"Why?" he asked.

"I mean, your real dad dies, later your mom dies, you move out on your own because your stepdad is no good. Then you work your butt off with nobody to help you, and then you lose your job…"

Leon thought about it. "I'm not mad at God. I don't think He had anything to do with the bad stuff. Just a minute," he said as he turned to shake hands with the pastor at the door of the church.

"Thanks for coming," the pastor said softly. He shook hands with Leon and his family.

"Thanks for the message," answered Leon.

The pastor turned to me. "Thanks for coming."

"Yeah. Thanks, Mr., I mean, Reverend, uh, sir."

When we stood outside, my parents got talking to some neighbors, and I pulled Leon aside again.

"You were saying?"

"Oh, yeah. Sure. I get tired sometimes. But hey, in a couple of years, Winnie and I will be old enough to take care of Sam legally by ourselves." Leon looked happy.

"You're crazy as a wedge. I'll help you all I can, but if it was me, I'd give up and probably steal to get by. I mean, if I had to get rent money and food and all that stuff. I'd probably break into cottages or something."

"You probably wouldn't." Leon looked at me again and still had that grin on his face. "I can't explain it all." He kicked at a piece of snow on the steps. "But a few days ago, it came to me that I'll make the rent money and the food money. I just know it will work out."

When I walked by their apartment door later that night, I could hear Winnie singing "I Wonder as I Wander," and I wished I was in there with them.

On New Year's Eve, I was watching TV in Leon's apartment when another envelope was put under the door. Zach did his work well: He delivered it on time, knocking once and getting out of sight by the time Leon ran into the hallway. There was fifty dollars this time, and Leon didn't seem as surprised.

"More money!" said Winnie.

Leon counted it out. "With what I earned shoveling and doing odd jobs, plus this, we have enough to pay rent and buy groceries. We're good for January. Now all I need is another good job that lasts a while. I wonder who is leaving this for us?"

Ricky's older brother, Mike, had gotten Leon's old job at the grocery store. The manager liked him at first because he had good manners and a charming way with the customers. He could be polite, like Ricky. But he lost the job a few weeks later when he was caught stealing from the store. He was charged by the police. I wondered how his mother would get him out of that one. My dad once told me a judge really gives it to someone who is caught stealing from their own employer.

School started again, and I fell into my routine of getting into trouble and doing as little work as possible. Leon continued to make the rounds after school, asking around for part-time jobs, but he got nothing regular. I kept my secret job at the GOOF. I always went in the back way, through the alley to the door beside the Dumpster. Though the GOOF was a popular restaurant, I was usually out of sight in the kitchen. When I took trays of dishes in and out, nobody in the dining area could see me because of a partition.

Then Winnie came in one day to pick up some take-out food for a family she was babysitting for. She caught me in the act. I had just finished bringing out a tray of steaming clean dishes. I picked up a tray of dirty dishes and turned to bang the door open with my butt when I saw her staring at me. Her jaw dropped when she saw me in a white apron—working. I almost dropped the tray, and I hid in the kitchen, wondering what to say.

When I peeked out the window in the kitchen door, she was waiting there with a grin, so I went out to talk to her.

"Don't tell anyone," I whispered.

"But this is so cool. Brandon with a job!"

"I'm serious. You'll wreck my image."

"You're not lazy as a fat dog after all," she laughed.

"Don't tell. Especially not Leon."

"Whatever you want. But I think it's cool. You working." She grinned again and left the restaurant with her take-out order.

On days I wasn't working at the restaurant, I felt restless. Working steadily gave me extra energy, and on my days off I didn't feel lazy anymore. I began seriously working on the dirt bike. It was cold outside, but my plan was to put it all together, get it running and try it out behind the apartment building, never mind the snow. I was starting to put tires on, and my mother wanted to know what all the noise was.

"Why are you grunting and shouting like that?" she asked.

"I'm trying to get these stupid tires on. I've borrowed the right tire lifters, and everything lines up, but I just can't—"

"Where's your soap?" she asked.

"What do you mean?"

"You need to get soapy water all over the rim and tire, Brandon."

"Who says?"

"Everyone knows that," she said. Everyone but me. It seemed like a dumb idea, but it was like getting Sam out of the pipe. So maybe…I waited until she was gone and tried it anyway. I smeared some soapy water on the tires and rims, and the tires popped on smooth and easy. There is something embarrassing about having your mom tell you how to put tires on your dirt bike. I wondered what else she knew, but I didn't feel like asking.

I worked on the bike alone in my room for hours, doing the last bits. I'd been given a motorcycle repair manual for Christmas, and I followed all the steps I could. I found spark plugs and plug wires tossed out behind the auto parts store. They were used but still looked good. The muffler had a crack in it, so I cut up a tin can and wrapped it around the cracked place and then used hose clamps to hold it on. My dad said that would do—for a while. The gas tank leaked from the part that led into the fuel-line switch thingy. But I found I could seal it with some pink silicone tape my dad had. The battery came from a dirt bike at the local wrecker. I was almost ready to take the bike out of my apartment.

"By the way," my mom said a few evenings later, "I was talking to Winnie down in the laundry room yesterday."

"Oh?" I said.

"She's such a nice girl. Anyway, she asked what you were doing with all the money you were making at the restaurant."

"What didja say?"

"I told her the truth. I said I haven't a clue. I told her you asked for a bunch of envelopes after your first paycheck, and we haven't seen you spend anything since."

"Aaww! Why did you go and tell her that?"

"Well, Brandon, you never tell us anything. All we can do is guess."

"No, I mean about the envelopes."

"It seemed so strange, that's all. What *are* you doing with all that money? Saving for a new dirt bike?"

Chapter Nineteen

Two days later, I was ready to take the bike out for a trial run. My plan was to sneak it out after dark on a day the super wasn't nosing around. He'd freak out if he saw me put a dirt bike in the elevator. My mom would be happy it was gone because she complained of gasoline smells stinking up the place. But I needed someone to help me get it into the elevator.

I knocked on Zach's door, but nobody was home there. A light was on in Leon's place, but Winnie said Leon was helping an old lady clean out her attic. Winnie looked up and down the hallway to see if anyone was around, and then she leaned close and gave me a big kiss on the cheek. I was shocked.

"Wha…what's that for?" I asked.

"For helping."

"Helping who?"

"Us. The money. Leon needs the break. Thanks."

I was dizzy when I walked down the hall. In one month, things had really changed for me. I had started working and following orders, I had become able to give stuff away, and now I had finally been kissed by a girl. A really pretty girl.

The next day Leon was home, and together we got the bike into the elevator. We lifted the front wheel up and wedged it into the back corner of the elevator so the door could close. A bit of oil started dripping out but I smeared it away with my shoe. I hoped nobody would get in the elevator and tell the superintendent. Winnie and Sam took the stairs so they could watch the big moment.

When we got to the first floor, I used the super's key to get the back door open, and we rolled the dirt bike out onto the rear loading dock. Leon helped me bring it down the concrete steps. I twisted the key in the ignition, and the lights came on.

I opened the choke. Two kicks of the starter and the bike began to do the uneven *ring-ding-ding* of a two-stroke engine. "Whooo-hah!" I shouted. Winnie and Sam cheered. My heart raced, and I grinned so wide my face hurt.

"You did it, Brandon! Your bike works." Leon slapped me on the back. I climbed on the bike, put it in gear and stalled. After a few more tries I got the clutch to come out evenly, and suddenly I was riding down the parking lot, a cool breeze blowing around my ears. I stopped at the end, wobbled through a turn and headed back again. I had taken a wrecked old bike and a bunch of parts and put it all together and made it work. It was like creating new life.

At school my only thoughts were of getting home to try the new bike in the fields behind our building. I doodled motorcycles, tires, engines and mufflers all over my notebook in math class.

"Where is Zach?" Mr. Fletcher asked. "Anyone seen Zach?" My daydreaming stopped. Zach again. This was the third day in a row he'd been absent. I told myself he was fine, but a picture of Zach with a black eye kept coming into my head. I chased those thoughts away with a vision of riding my dirt bike through the fields. But the thoughts about Zach intruded. Just like I can tell if someone is going to punch with his left or his right, I knew something was wrong. I had to check on Zach.

I got kicked out of class in time to hear the secretary make her phone calls. I was counting on getting second-hand information when Zach himself came in wearing new shoes and new clothes. He was with an older woman I didn't recognize. Zach looked at me and gave me a shy grin. He didn't say anything. He looked tidier, but his hair still stuck up at the back. Zach and the woman went into the office to see Mr. Sitzer and were in there a long time. When they came out, the woman told Mrs. Miller that Zach would be back at school the next day. She leaned closer to the secretary and whispered to her. I was pretending to tattoo myself with a Bic pen and trying hard to hear at the same time, but I couldn't catch any of it. The secretary got out the student information binder and make some changes. Then Zach and the woman left.

"Ah, can I go back now? I'm bored," I said.

"Brandon, you stay until Mr. Sitzer says you can leave."

"But I'm just wasting time here. I feel like disturbing a class somewhere."

"Brandon! You know the rules."

So I just sat there, as usual. It was nice to see Zach looking well cared for. I was beginning to think that maybe good things could happen after all. Zach had always deserved better than he got from his dad. I hoped that if I was ever a dad, I would treat my son better than Zach's weasel-faced father treated him. Maybe I'd treat my son like…like Leon treated Sam.

I remembered what Leon had said that night after church—that somehow he knew things were going to work out. I found myself hoping desperately that he was right.

Chapter Twenty

"Did you hear about Zach?" Melissa asked me the next day. Melissa was the chat-room queen—she always knew all the latest gossip. "He's in a foster home. Children's Aid took him away from his dad."

"Never heard a thing about it," I said.

"You need to go online more often. The chat rooms are full of information."

The chat rooms were buzzing with other rumors too. Rumors started spreading about Leon and Winnie and Sam. Kids stopped talking when one of them came near.

"I hear their dad is in jail, and they're keeping it secret," Melissa said.

"I've seen their dad lots of times," I lied, but my version didn't travel.

Leon and Winnie were quieter than usual. Winnie didn't laugh as much, and she stayed apart from her friends during recess breaks. Only Sam was the same, active as ever.

I asked Leon if everything was all right, even though I already knew it wasn't.

"We might have to call Fred Prentice again, maybe move to Springfield or some other town," Leon told me.

"Why?"

"One of the neighbors phoned the school and said she thought something was wrong. She's been watching the hallway, and she's sure she hasn't seen our 'daddy' in a long time. Sitzer asked me about it."

"What did you say?"

"The usual lies. Dad works nights. The phone's out of service. His work number changed and I don't know what it is…"

"Did he believe you?"

"I don't think so. He's heard it all before. Brandon, if we're gone some morning, you'll know we've moved on. You can have our TV and anything else you want."

"You're moving?"

"I haven't decided. But if we do, it will happen fast. You've been our best friend. I won't forget what you did for us."

"Does Winnie think you should move?" I asked.

"She really likes it here and would hate to leave. But she knows sooner or later they're going to come to our place and check us out. We haven't told Sam yet. I don't want him to worry. He's still a kid."

The Children's Aid came sooner rather than later. Leon was out looking for work. A man and a woman walked into the apartment building. The woman was the same one I had seen in the office with Zach. They got the super from his apartment, and then they all went to the elevator. I followed them into the elevator and sauntered past when they stopped at Leon's apartment door. I waited around a corner where I could hear what was going on without being seen.

They knocked a few times.

"Open up, please. It's Children's Aid," said the man.

"Open up. We have the legal right to come in," said the woman. Finally I heard the sound of a key in the lock. It must have been the super's passkey.

"We're coming in," said the woman.

The door opened, and all I heard was Sam shouting, "You can't come in here!" and Winnie crying.

I felt like I had been kicked in the gut. The superintendent left, glaring at me as he passed by.

After about half an hour the apartment door opened. The woman from Children's Aid led the way to the elevator. The man walked behind the kids. Winnie carried a suitcase; she was still crying and angry. Sam was silent and looked ill. He carried a green garbage bag full of stuff. I stood by the elevator door pretending I was waiting for the elevator.

"Our family is better than anything you could come up with," Winnie snarled at them. She stopped talking when she noticed me. I winked at her, hoping she would guess that I had a plan.

When the elevator came, we all got in, and I moved to the back where the rear door was. All the others turned to face the front door. Sam was sniffling. He turned to look at me, and I shook my head a little and put my finger to my lips.

As we neared the ground floor, I got the super's elevator key from my pocket and, using my body to hide what I was doing, put it into the service lock facing the rear door. When we reached the first floor, I clicked it into the out-of-service position. Behind us, the back doors slid open at the same time the front doors did. I jumped forward and pushed myself between Winnie and Sam and the Children's Aid people.

"Everybody out!" I shouted, pushing the man and woman into the lobby. "Run, Winnie! Sam! Run!" I yelled over my shoulder. They hesitated a moment, and then Sam, followed by Winnie, ran out the back elevator door and onto the loading dock behind the building. The man was too surprised to react, but the woman tried to shove me aside and go after Winnie and Sam.

"You're interfering with a legal order," she shouted at me.

"I don't care," I said, grunting as she grabbed me by the elbow.

"You could be charged under the Criminal Code!"

"So charge me," I shouted.

The man was pudgy and soft, like my old teddy bear. He watched us scuffle, wringing his hands and muttering, "Oh, this is all so unpleasant…"

"Go get those kids, Alex!" shouted the woman. He took off around the corner just as I managed to get out of the woman's clutches.

"Sorry, lady. Gotta go!" I said. I saw Winnie's head disappearing past a small rise in a field behind our building. I ran off in another direction, yelling their names, hoping to lead the Children's Aid people in the wrong direction.

It didn't work. The wispy man had seen the kids. I heard later that Winnie and Sam tried to outrun them but had to give up when the police came. Meanwhile, another police officer came and waited in the apartment for Leon to arrive. I hung around the lobby for an hour to warn him, but Leon must have come in the side door and gone up the stairs. He didn't see me. He was taken by surprise in his own place, the place he called home, an apartment with mismatched furniture and kids' shoes in the cupboard.

The last I saw of Leon, he was walking, head down and shoulders slumped, beside a big police officer. The cop held his hand lightly but steadily on Leon's shoulder, ready for any new attempt at freedom. But I could see Leon had given up. His family was caught. He was put into the back of the police car like some kind of criminal, and the cruiser drove away.

Chapter Twenty-One

Rumors flew. The whole town talked about how Leon and Winnie and Sam had been living without a father or mother. Some said the father had run out on them. Some said he was a drug dealer. Others said he was in jail. People guessed the kids were runaways from the United States. People who knew the least had the most opinions. I kept silent.

When my dad heard the rumors, he sat me down for a talk. I admitted to knowing all about it and helping them. He was mad at me for not having told him. "This isn't the kind of thing you keep secret," he said.

"I promised not to rat them out. Would you have me rat out a friend?"

"Of course not, but this isn't someone stealing a chocolate bar. That boy was taking responsibility for a ten-year-old and a twelve-year-old. And he is only thirteen himself. It's dangerous. Anything could have happened."

"And you would have turned them in?" I asked.

"Maybe we could have helped them, taken them in ourselves," he said.

"You always tell me we can't afford stuff. How could we have taken them in?"

"Brandon, these are your friends. We could have found a way to help. Now who knows what will happen? How long did it take the authorities to help your buddy Zach?"

"Years?" I guessed.

"That's right! Once the government gets involved, everything takes forever. Now Leon's family will have to be put somewhere."

"Where?" I asked.

"Who knows? Foster care, probably. Kids can't live on their own. It's against the law."

"Leon was always afraid they'd split them up. Send Sam to one family and Winnie to another."

"I don't know what they will do—but I know if you had told us earlier, we might have been able to help them," answered my dad.

"They were doing fine, until…"

"Until what?"

"Until Leon lost his job. He was holding it all together."

"Leon is a minor. He's not allowed to live on his own and take care of his family. That's ridiculous."

"They do it in poor countries. Kids whose parents die of AIDS, in Africa. They manage all the time."

"This is Canada," my dad said.

"Don't you have a friend at the newspaper?" I asked.

"Luke Hendry? Yes, why?"

"I think if people heard how hard Leon worked to pay the rent and buy the groceries and stay out of trouble, they would be proud of him, not arrest them and try to put them with strangers."

"The kids are safe now. They won't be harmed—"

"Leon kept them from harm! Now they'll get split up. He was a better parent than a lot of kids have!"

"But Leon's just a kid..." Dad still sounded doubtful, but he seemed to be listening to me.

"But if people find out how well they managed, maybe it would be okay. Leon always did his homework for school, and so did Winnie, and they both kept Sam out of trouble. They deserve a medal, not to be taken away and put in foster care. They're not like Zach."

My dad frowned and tapped his fingers on the armrest of his recliner. "The sister, Winnie, didn't she babysit for a lot of people in the building? I heard she'd wash people's dishes and clean up after their kids without being asked."

"She did. And even Sam, who always gets in trouble, took a paper route to help pay for food and stuff. They never wasted their money on junk food or electronics or movies."

"Hmmmm. Leave this with me," said my dad.

Chapter Twenty-Two

Leon's apartment remained dark. Nobody knew where they were until one of Winnie's friends got a quick phone call. They were living in a hotel in Springfield, with workers keeping an eye on them in case they ran away again. That was all Winnie was allowed to say. The hotel had a swimming pool, cable TV and all sorts of cool stuff, but they missed their place in Kingsville and wanted to go back.

The next week, Leon and Winnie and Sam still had not come back to school.

"Where are Leon and Winnie and Sam?" I asked Mr. Sitzer.

"Why were you sent down today, Brandon?" he asked.

"Hey, I wasn't sent down. I just want to know what happened to Leon and Winnie and Sam."

"I really can't tell you, Brandon, but I'm sure they will be fine."

"They were fine before," I replied.

"They will be taken care of properly, by adults."

"But they took care of themselves properly."

"Leon is underage, so is Winnie. They aren't responsible."

"They were responsible. I watched them every day."

"And are you a good judge of responsibility, Brandon?" said Mr. Sitzer with a smile.

The remark hurt. "Leon was a better dad than most dads I know."

Mr. S. changed the subject and reminded me about my behavior. Then he sent me back to the classroom.

The next day an article about Leon's family appeared in our local newspaper. The article asked why nobody had noticed these kids living without parents. As far as I could tell, the article blamed the school, the apartment superintendent and Leon's former employer for not realizing what was going on. It also praised Leon and Winnie for being responsible young people. Then a TV station from Springfield mentioned in its 6:00 PM news broadcast how Leon had outwitted most of the town of Kingsville. Reporters from bigger daily newspapers came to town to find out more about the story.

A newspaper photograph showed Leon wearing new clothes. A caption under it said *Older brother pleads for his family not to be split up*.

Another newspaper showed the three of them standing on the steps of a courthouse after a Family Court judge had reviewed their situation. The article said that several witnesses had come in to testify on behalf of the George children, including two teachers from their school and several neighbors in their apartment building. The judge was studying the matter, and he would rule the following week. Meanwhile, the newspaper said, the family was living in a hotel, and a private tutor was coming in to make sure they didn't fall behind in their schoolwork. The newspaper stories began to call Leon a hero. They talked about his well-developed sense of responsibility and duty to his family. Others said that many men could learn from Leon what it takes to be a good father.

At school, people like Ricky started saying how they suspected all along that Leon was doing this. Leon was "cool" all of a sudden. Their hero.

Television reporters following another lead found Leon's stepdad in Toronto and shouted questions at him when he answered the door.

"Why did you allow the three George children to leave without notifying authorities?"

"Why didn't you try to track them down?"

"Are you being charged with neglect?"

The stepfather swore at them and slammed the door.

My reading skills got better as the unhappy story unraveled. Every day more details came out about my best friends. The newspapers hinted that the stepfather would be charged soon but could not say what the charges were.

The reporters said Leon had done the right thing in leaving an abusive situation but that he should have notified the authorities. A lawyer spoke for Leon's family and said they were not allowed to discuss the matter.

The papers also found old Fred Prentice, the man who had been posing as their father. He was interviewed on TV.

"Why did you help keep their secret?"

He stared with bloodshot eyes at the camera. "Maybe it was against the law," he rasped, "but I've known Leon since he was a little boy. I trust him. Leon was afraid he and Winnie and Sam would be split up, and I thought he was right."

"Why didn't you take care of them yourself?"

"I'm an alcoholic. I can barely take care of myself."

"Will you be charged with being an accessory to the neglect of underage children?"

"If I do, I'll serve my time. I believe I did the right thing," he said.

Finally the reporters interviewed the Children's Aid workers who had come to get them.

"We have reviewed the situation thoroughly, interviewing teachers and neighbors who knew them best…"

My dad and I looked at each other and laughed. Nobody had asked me, and I knew them better than anybody.

"We have made a recommendation to the court. We treat every case individually. We have decided to recommend an exception to the usual rules. Leon George has proved himself, along with his sister, Winnie, to be a mature and reliable caregiver. He has been an exceptional parent for his sister and brother.

"They will be allowed to live as they have lived for the last eight months—independently. Our workers will check with them weekly, and the ministry will make a very rare exception and give them family benefits and financial assistance. The George family will not be split up or sent to a foster home. They can continue to live on their own in Kingsville."

Chapter Twenty-Three

The party at Leon's apartment was something I'll never forget. It was the loudest celebration we'd ever had in the building. Neighbors, Winnie's babysitting families and children, social workers, Children's Aid workers, policemen, Mrs. Cawfield and Mr. Fletcher all showed up to help them celebrate. Even the Family Court judge and one of the lawyers came. One family brought a big CD-DVD player and speakers they weren't using, plugged it in and left it there for Leon's family. Other people brought clothing and gifts. Someone brought a good used barbecue for their balcony and steaks to cook on it. Despite the cold weather, Mr. Fletcher stood out on the balcony and grilled steaks and burgers and chicken. He called Leon his "Honorary Top Fletchville Student." He said he never thought he would teach a kid who was already using the lessons.

Envelopes with money in them were left on the kitchen table. Some had instructions on them: *To be used only for movies and taxi fare to the theater. Enjoy.* Another said *For three fancy meals at the GOOF,* and there were more envelopes that just said *To Leon* or *To Winnie* or *To Sam*. There was music and laughter and singing. Zach came with his social worker and foster mother, whom he really seemed to like. He seemed to be less afraid of people now that his dad was out of his life.

At one point I overheard Leon saying to the social worker, "I'm glad you helped Zach. He needed to get out of his house. But our situation was different. I hope you understand why I did what I did. Friends?"

"As I told the judge," said the woman, "you did what you needed to do, and I understand that now. We were both just doing our jobs. Friends," she said, giving him an awkward hug.

Adults served the food to Winnie and Sam and Leon, who were told to sit down and enjoy the meal. They'd earned it and for once they could relax and enjoy themselves.

Sometime during the evening, one of the neighbors, a guy with a haircut like Elvis, got everyone to be quiet. He said he wanted to say something. He began by telling us how sweet Winnie was when she babysat his kids, how she looked after them so well and made them behave but still allowed them to have fun.

"She even cleaned up the kitchen and living room so that we would come home to a nice tidy apartment. We don't have a lot of money to help you with, but you have our friendship and our respect. Leon, I don't know you as well, but I see what you've done with your family. You've been able to create a good home for your brother and sister. When I was your age, I was stealing cars."

There were more speeches and people saying thanks. Then Sam came forward with an envelope and presented it to Leon.

"Our real father died when I was little," he said. "In the last few years, whenever I got into trouble, I had Leon to turn to. He was strict with me, but he was fair, I guess." He stopped and looked down. "I was bad lots of times. I got into trouble when Leon told me I should keep my mouth shut and my fists in my pockets." Some of the people laughed. Sam went on. "Sometimes we were almost found out, like when I got caught in the sewer pipe. But Leon never made me feel like I wasn't special or wasn't wanted or that I was too much trouble. He would play catch with me and teach me how to throw, even after I'd done something wrong."

Sam scratched his leg. "I just gave Leon a Father's Day card," he continued. "I had to ask the manager of the variety store to look in his back room because it isn't time for Father's Day yet. But it's time for me to give him this card. To Leon. He's my brother, but he's also been like a father. Happy Father's Day."

"I signed it too!" shouted Winnie. Leon opened his card and gave his brother a friendly punch in the arm. There were more speeches and more congratulations.

At some point in the evening, the manager at the grocery store came to the party, and everyone listened and cheered as he told Leon his company was willing to make an exception and give him his old job back, even though he was only thirteen. "We'd be proud to have you back," he said.

"I might not need to work as many hours as I used to," Leon said. "The government is going to help us with money. But it wouldn't feel right not earning some money. I'll take the job," he said. "Thanks," he added.

Then Leon looked around and motioned everyone to be quiet. He had another announcement to make, he said. He pointed to me and introduced me to everyone as his best friend.

"I've learned that people aren't always what you think they are. I thought Brandon wasn't very smart. In fact, I thought he was dumb and kind of crazy. He isn't—crazy, I mean. Or stupid. He's a lot smarter than he likes people to believe." Leon grinned at me. "And he's great to have on your side in a fight. One of the hardest things was always telling lies to people. But I knew I had to. But when I met Brandon and learned more about him, I knew I could trust him with our secret. He was the only person I ever told about our situation. He's known for months…"

There was some whispering, and everyone looked at me.

Leon continued. "Brandon deserved to be told because he was also looking out for us, the way he looks out for people—in secret. He does things for people, not to be thanked, but because they need to be done. When I lost my job, Brandon started working. He never told me about it, but all of a sudden money started coming under the door late at night, when Brandon just 'happened' to be visiting. I figured he was having someone else put the money under the door so I wouldn't suspect him."

"You told him!" I pointed at Winnie, laughing.

"I did not," she insisted.

"I figured it out myself," said Leon. "You aren't the only person in town who knows how to follow people and not be seen. In the first week I followed you to work twice."

It was my turn to be surprised.

"I knew you were working at the GOOF and that you didn't want me to know. So I left some flour on the floor in front of our door one Friday night when I thought another envelope might come under the door. The envelope came that night. I followed the flour to Zach's apartment."

Zach looked guilty as everyone turned to look at him.

"He wouldn't admit to anything either," Leon said. "He only told me he didn't know what was in the envelopes. He wouldn't tell me who had given them to him, but I knew by then it was you."

"Way to go, Brandon! Way to go, Zach!" people shouted. Others whistled. Winnie grinned at me.

"I want to pay you back, Brandon, for your cash donations to the George family." Leon pulled an envelope stuffed with bills out of his pocket.

"Uh, I can't take it back," I said.

"Sure you can. You earned it," insisted Leon.

"No, I meant it when I gave it, and I want you guys to have it."

"That's the kind of friend he is," said Leon. Everyone cheered. I went red.

Next, Winnie's music teacher stood up. He was a thin man with a sandy beard and glasses.

"There are other secrets all you people should know about," he said. "Leon came to me way back in October and asked for guitar lessons for Winnie." Everyone turned to look at Winnie, who looked surprised. "When I told Leon they were twenty dollars per lesson, he said they couldn't afford that." Winnie's jaw dropped. "Leon offered to work for me every week to pay for part of the lessons if I would take Winnie on. The deal was—and Leon insisted on it— that Winnie would pay five dollars for the lessons, and I would tell her that was the real price. He did not want her to know what he was doing."

"Leon, you did that?" Winnie jumped up. "I love you!" Winnie gave her brother a big hug. "All that time I never knew you were helping me."

The music teacher then offered Winnie free music lessons for the next year. "If I'd known you guys were earning your own food and rent money, I would have done it sooner," he said.

The party carried on like that, with more details of who had fooled who. Though we all laughed to hear it, it was always clear to me that it had all been serious business for them. One mistake or a few questions from authorities could have exposed them long ago.

"We're so glad we don't have to pretend anymore," said Leon. Winnie and Sam shouted their agreement.

As we were going down to our apartment, my dad said, "You were right, Brandon."

"Right about what?"

"Right to help. Right to keep your friend's secret."

Dad reached out and slapped me on the back, hard.

"Thanks, Dad," I said.

René Schmidt didn't do too well in school because he was too busy making up stories in his head. As a young man he traveled in Europe and North America by bicycle and motorcycle, worked in a nickel mine, drove taxis and trucks, did construction work and worked on a Great Lakes freighter. René is an honors graduate of York University's creative writing program. He is married with two sons and lives in Brighton, Ontario, where he is a teacher. He has written three books on Canadian disasters. This is his first novel.